True to

Her Faith

Classic Stories

True to Her Faith

A STORY OF FRANCE IN THE TIME OF THE HUGUENOTS

Narrated by Helen. G.

CHRISTIAN FOCUS PUBLICATIONS

This edition © copyright 2006
Christian Focus Publications
ISBN: 1-84550-220-5

Published by
Christian Focus Publications
Geanies House, Fearn, Tain, Ross-shire,
IV20 1TW, Scotland, Great Britain.
www. christianfocus. com
email: info@christianfocus. com
Originally published by London; Gall and Inglis, 25 Paternoster
Square: And Edinburgh.

Cover Illustration by Jean Baptiste Camille Corot
Inside Illustrations by Shona MacDonald
Cover Design by Dannie van Stratten
Printed and Bound in Denmark
by Nørhaven Paperback A/S

CONTENTS

PREFACE

Many years ago, as a child this tale was often repeated to me by an aged relative. I never wearied with the repetition; and I think much of the charm which surrounded that tale was attributed to the fact, that the character of 'Suzanne de l'Orme,' and the sufferings she went through during the earlier part of her life, were no fiction. She actually suffered and endured patiently all the trials and temptations which I have described: and she was as good and amiable as she was patient.

The dear relative, to whom I have alluded, saw Mademoiselle de l'Orme; and her eldest brother and she counted it as a privilege to claim even a remote relationship with so heroic and high-minded a woman. Many a twilight hour, both in summer time and beside the ruddy glow of the winter fire, was beguiled and made pleasant both to myself and my sisters. When tired out with the day's lessons, and wearied with play, we clustered round 'Grandmamma,' coaxing her to tell us a story. Sometimes, perhaps, our tempers were somewhat ruffled, and we did not feel quite in charity with each other – at such times the simple recital of little Suzanne's sufferings soothed, what seemed to us, great worries – worries which soon sank into insignificance by comparison, and which, when the tale was ended, were scarcely thought of or remembered.

I have nephews and nieces of my own now, and they have derived the same pleasure and instruction from the recital, which we did in our youthful days. In a pleasant cottage, some twenty miles north of Carlisle, little folks have often come with a request, that 'Aunt Helen' would tell them all she could remember about the brave little girl who is the heroine of the tale; and my eldest niece, Rose Arnold, suggested my writing out the incidents connected with it, for the especial benefit of all my young relatives.

Acting on that suggestion, and ensconced in the cosy morning room of that pleasant cottage, I have penned the story which fills the following pages. The sunlight streaming in at the open lattice, birds twittering in the branches of the surrounding trees, and the air filled with the delicious perfume of numberless flowers growing in the garden which my favourite window overlooks, brought back my childhood's impressions so vividly, that I seemed to hear that true tale 'o'er again. ' Rose, of course, was seated opposite to me whilst I wrote, generally engaged with a sketch of one of the lovely views with which this neighbourhood abounds. Ever and anon, however, her inquiring eyes were directed towards me, to see if my work progressed. She has been very patient. Day after day she has sat there expectant; but now my task is done, and her watching ended.

Partial friends induced me to publish the little Huguenot tale, thinking that other children will perchance derive as much pleasure from its perusal as those dear to me have done. In the hope that it will meet with an indulgent and kindly reception from the public in general, I commit it to its fate, and trust that those who read it will find it as pleasant a task as I have had in writing it.

H. G.

A Quiet Village

Many, very many years ago, in the outskirts of a quiet village, situated near the town of Saumur, in France, stood a quaint looking house; its high-pitched roof, and curiously twisted chimneys, bore witness to its antiquity, as well as the chequered woodwork, which crossed and re-crossed its somewhat dilapidated exterior. It has evidently resisted the storms of long past years, and at the time of which we write, was falling gradually into decay. Still, there was an air of neatness about it, and about the little plot of garden which divided it from the high road, that said much in favour of its occupants.

The persons who inhabited this house were Protestants, or Huguenots, as they were then called; and the family consisted of a father, mother, and their five children, the eldest of whom, Suzanne, is the heroine of our tale. Monsieur de l'Orme had inherited his house from his father, a country gentleman of moderate fortune, who had brought up his only son in the faith he had himself received from his ancestors. Pierre de l'Orme had amply repaid the care bestowed on his early training, and was a truly religious and conscientious man, respected and beloved by all who knew him. At the time our story begins, he was about forty years of age; tall and slight in figure, with a dark complexion and regular features. His wife was some years younger, and although her character was very different to his, yet never were two people so thoroughly suited to each other. Monsieur de l'Orme was of a thoughtful turn of mind, which was greatly increased by the troubled times in which he lived; whilst his wife, naturally merry and cheerful, tended to enliven a disposition which might have become morose, but for her pleasing influence. She was quite different to him also in personal appearance; in early youth she had been very beautiful, and even now, as she sat engaged in some household task, she was very fair to look upon. With an extremely delicate complexion, hair of the palest brown, and an ever-varying expression of countenance, you could scarcely have fancied her old enough to be the wife of the grave man who entered the room where she sat.

This room was large and low, panelled with oak. It ran across one end of the house, and was lighted up by long narrow windows at each end. The floor, black with age, was carefully polished; and the old well-worn furniture carried one's thoughts back to times gone by.

Madame de l'Orme, as she sat by the open window, in a curiously carved high-backed chair, cushioned with crimson velvet, looked like an old picture. She was dressed in the fashion of the time, which was at once quaint and picturesque; a robe of soft, rich brown silk fell around her in massive and graceful folds; cut square in the bodice, it was relieved by a snowy kerchief, fastened with a gold pin at the throat; the sleeves which only reached just below the elbow, were finished by deep ruffles of lace, and her fair features were shaded by a cap of the same delicate material. Very curious in shape it was; high in the crown, and brought forward so as almost to touch her forehead; it was fastened back at either side of the head, so as to form two long broad lappets, which reached the shoulder on each side. An apron of embroidered muslin completed her costume.

As she sat mechanically pursuing her task, her soft blue eyes were often filled with tears, which fell in spite of herself on the work she held in her hand. It was a hot afternoon in the month of August. Not the slightest breeze stirred the leaves on the surrounding trees; and the very insects seemed to have gone to sleep, wearied by the intensity of the heat. Nothing was heard but the ticking of the old clock, which marked the hours as they slowly passed away. At length a well-known step was heard on the gravel path; and Madame de l'Orme started up to greet her husband as he entered, exclaiming eagerly, 'Well, Pierre?'

'My poor Madeleine!' he replied, 'I have no news for you; I have been again unsuccessful. '

With a cry of anguish she fell back on her seat, and for some moments seemed a prey to the most uncontrollable grief; all at once she remembered her husband, and stifling her sobs, she looked up with a faint smile, and said, 'Pierre, how selfish I am!'

'No, Madeleine! You are not selfish, your grief is natural. Mine too is great, almost too great to bear, except that I know that it is God who sends the trial. '

The better to understand the foregoing conversation, we must go back many years; and, moreover, trace an outline of events which belongs to history.

THE HUGUENOTS

After the massacre of St. Bartholomew in the reign of Charles IX. , king of France, Henry IV. , then king of Navarre, himself a Huguenot (having been brought up in that faith by his pious mother, Jeanne d'Albret), was obliged, on ascending the throne of France, after the death of Henry III. , to abjure his religion, and become, as a matter of necessity, a member of the Romish faith.

He, however, never forgot the friends of his early years, and was always careful of the interests of those of his subjects who professed and practised the Reformed religion. He granted them great privileges, and allowed them to worship God according to their creed and conscience, in whatever part of his dominions they might be settled. Moreover, fearing that his successors might not have the same kindly feelings towards the Huguenots as he had, he gave them several fortified towns and strongholds in various parts of his kingdom, so that they might defend themselves against their oppressors in the event of a persecution. Finally, he confirmed all these grants and concessions, by issuing and promulgating in 1598, an edict, commonly known as the famous 'Edict of Nantes.'

After this the Huguenots lived in peace for many years; but after Henry's death, troubles arose. One by one their privileges were taken from them; first one thing and then another, till at last Louis XIV revoked the edict which had so long protected them, and they were again at the mercy of their foes. It was an iniquitous act, and one which cost Louis very dear; for thousands of his subjects fled from his kingdom, and carried their industry and knowledge of manufactures, for which the French were then famous, to other and more tolerant countries. Others, however, struggled on, hoping for better times; amongst these were the immediate ancestors of the de l'Ormes. So far they had not suffered to any grievous extent; they had been left comparatively in peace, and, with the exception of fines, extortions, and other petty annoyances, they had no reason to complain.

The Chancellor of France in those days was Michel le Tellier, a very old man, and a bigoted Roman Catholic; he died in 1685, and his last request to his sovereign was, that the 'Edict of Nantes' should be revoked, and the Huguenots exposed to the most rigorous persecution, to make them return to the bosom of his beloved Church. Some writers are of the opinion that le Tellier advocated the repression of Protestantism from conscientious motives; that he thought he was really doing God's service, and advancing the interests of the Romish faith, by extirpating what was then called heresy, and punishing those whose views differed from his. And it is recorded by these writers, that when his dying wish was granted, he thanked God devoutly, actually using the beautiful words of the aged Simeon, when he beheld the infant Saviour of the world for the first time in the Temple. By others, far less pure and exalted motives are ascribed to the Chancellor, and his character is portrayed in any thing but an advantageous light. At this distance of time, it is hardly possible to arrive at a just conclusion on the matter; but it is a certain fact, that he urged his royal master, by every argument in his power, to adopt the severest measures towards his Huguenot subjects.

Being moreover encouraged and worked upon by his minister Louvois, who was the son of le Tellier, and far more unscrupulous and cruel than his father, Louis the XIV. , entered eagerly into the plan of persecution. He hated his Protestant subjects, because of the difference between his religious opinions and theirs; but it was not so much this feeling of hatred which actuated him in adopting these severe measures (for in reality it did not matter much to him what their religion was), as his insane wish to maintain uniformity in every thing, no matter what, whether creeds or politics, or even in much less important subjects, and he therefore heartily concurred in every scheme which would tend to establish his favourite theory.

Accordingly, on the 2nd of October, 1685, the deed was signed, which has cast an undying shadow in the memory of Louis the Great. This deed condemned hundreds of thousands of the mistaken monarch's unoffending subjects to torture, death, exile, and apostasy; for many — an almost incredible number, complied with the wishes of their king, and abjured the Protestant for the Roman Catholic faith, thereby obtaining pardon for former errors, and immunity from farther persecution. But these wretched people, in many cases, indeed in most of them, were not sincere in their profession of Catholicism. They outwardly conformed to the ordinances of the Church they had been compelled to enter, but secretly, in their homes, they worshipped God after the manner of their fathers. It was indeed in fear and trembling they did so, for discovery would have entailed fiercer punishment. They had given up their faith from various motives — some to preserve their possessions, some for the sake of having their children restored to them, others from cowardice, and many because they had no fixed principles, and it was a matter of indifference to them what creed they professed, so long as they were left in peace. It has been computed that four hundred thousand persons, guilty of no other crime than differing in religious belief from their other fellow subjects, perished in the crusade organized against them, whilst an equal number found refuge in flight. Troops, chiefly dragoons, were spread over the face of the country, hence the name of 'Dragonnades,' by which the cruel massacres which they perpetrated were called, and many a fair town and hamlet in Normandy, Brittany, Provence, Languedoc, and other parts were made desolate, and ravaged by fire and sword. By the unheard of cruelties of these soldiers, at least one-fourth of the kingdom was depopulated, and the country abandoned to pillage; and as soon as the revocation of the 'Edict' was signed, the Protestant Churches were destroyed, the schools closed, and terror and desolation were spread over the land. Such was the state of things at the time our story begins. At that period the aspect of affairs was very gloomy; an event had occurred about a month before, which had terrified, and almost paralysed, the whole of the Protestant community of that district.

Suzanne de l'Orme, a girl of twelve years of age, had been sent by her mother some distance from the village where they lived, on an errand of charity. The way was lonely, but she had traversed it before; and although so young a child, she was perfectly fearless. She had not, however, been subjected to any very great trial yet, but the time was not very distant when her fortitude was to be put to the test. She was a grave and quiet child, and thoughtful beyond her years; but she inherited her mother's sweetness of disposition, and was so affectionate in her manner as to be almost idolized by her family. To strangers she was not so attractive as a more lively child would have been; but when her amiable character was understood, she was much beloved. Suzanne had heard so much of the troubles, which those who professed the Reformed faith were called upon to endure, that insensibly she brooded over them, and the remembrance of what she had been told, left a deep impression on her childish mind.

It was the custom of the Huguenots to instil the principles of their religion into their children's minds as soon as they could understand anything; and the quiet, sedate, and even austere manner of their daily life was such, that, as they grew up, they retained the impressions then given. This was the case with little Suzanne. Although her parents were far less stern than most of the Protestants who lived in those times, still they carefully explained their religious tenets to their children, and assured themselves that they really understood what they had been at such pains to teach them.

On the day of which we now write, she walked slowly along with her little basket on her arm, and as she walked, she thought of many things; but somehow the image of her parents, of her brothers and sisters, haunted her continually. Her mind was perpetually recurring to the many little pleasures she had enjoyed with them, to the kindnesses she had received at their hands, and still it seemed as if she had a presentiment of evil. She thought of the troubles which might be in store for them, and a tinge of sadness was mingled with her pleasant imaginings.

At last old Nanette's cottage was reached, and she laid down the contents of her basket near the sick woman's couch, at the same time giving her a kind message from her mother.

'Madame is very good, Mademoiselle Suzanne, and I hope you will tell her how thankful I am for all her kindness. But, Mademoiselle, I wish you would not come so far by yourself; I am afraid something will happen to you. '

'Oh, Nanette! What could happen to me?'

'I do not know, Mademoiselle, but there are strange rumours afloat about our people, and I am afraid we shall not be left much longer in peace. I wish Adrien were here, for I would send him with you; but he went away early this morning with Angelique, to work on Monsieur Bontemp's farm, and I do not expect them home till sunset. '

'Oh! Never mind, my good Nanette, do not be uneasy about me. I am going away now, for my mother told me not to be long; so, good bye, and when I come again, I hope to find you stronger. '

'Adieu, Mademoiselle! I shall be very glad to hear you have reached home in safety. '

'Why, Nanette!' the little girl replied laughingly, 'you will succeed in making a coward of me if I stay longer, so I must really run away;' and with another pleasant 'good-bye', she departed homewards.

She went on for sometime without meeting any one; at last, on entering a long narrow lane, she saw a man on the other side of the low hedge, and fancied he looked at her with a peculiar expression of countenance. He also appeared to be keeping pace with her; at another moment she would scarcely have noticed this, but old Nanette's words seemed to be ringing in her ears, and she began to feel a certain degree of fear. Increasing her pace until she almost ran, Suzanne still endeavoured to keep calm; and as the man never uttered a word, she felt a little reassured.

At length the lane came to an end. As Suzanne turned into the high road, she suddenly stood face to face with two priests, who, observing her startled look, asked her civilly, 'what was the matter?'

She told them what had occurred; at the same time adding, she had been very silly, for the man was gone, and had not probably intended to frighten her.

The priests said it was very likely; but as she still seemed very much agitated, they told her they would willingly go back with her to the entrance of the village were they not obliged to keep an appointment at the convent of St. Anne. It was only a short distance from where they stood, and if she would accompany them thither, they would not be long about the business they were going to transact, and she should then have the advantage of their protection until she reached home, as they must pass her father's house on their way to theirs.

The little girl thanked them very much, but said she thought she ought to go home then as it was getting late, and she had quite got over her alarm. The man was no longer to be seen, and she was sure there was little else for her to fear; the two priests, however, pressed her so kindly to accompany them, that she finally yielded to their persuasion, less reluctantly than she would have done had she not known them well before; for she often met them in the village, and they were on as friendly terms with her father, as persons of such opposite opinions could be.

Poor Suzanne little knew it was a premeditated plan, and that she was never more to see her happy home again, and so she went with them unsuspectingly.

The idea of entrapping Huguenot children, for the purpose of converting them to the Roman Catholic religion, had long been in contemplation; but no attempt had been made to carry out the idea. Suzanne de l'Orme was destined to be the first victim of this infamous arrangement. Her father being a person of some note in the part of France where he lived, it was thought that a triumph would be obtained, if a child of his could be made to accept the Roman Catholic religion, instead of the one in which they had been brought up in. For some weeks this had been a settled thing, and the promoters of the plan were only waiting for a good opportunity to carry it out.

Some of their spies, having found out that Suzanne had been sent to the old woman's cottage, at once gave information to their employers. The priests, who had the spiritual charge of the village in which she lived, immediately conceived the idea of waylaying her, and carrying her to some place, where they could try the force of their arguments at their leisure, and without molestation. They knew that whilst she was with her parents, there was not the slightest chance of success for them; but they fancied, that away from their influence, and inside the convent walls, the task would be comparatively easy.

Accordingly, the man who frightened Suzanne by his strange behaviour, did so by their orders; and they were ready to seize their prize at the right moment, having foreseen what would be the result of their experiment.

When they arrived at St. Anne's, they were ushered into the convent parlour, and the Supérieure having been summoned, the priests told her what had happened, and begged that their young friend might be allowed to remain until they were ready to accompany her home.

The lady at once assented, and after a few minutes conversation, she went out with the priests at their request, leaving Suzanne alone in the cool and quiet room, and in truth she was by no means sorry of the rest she enjoyed, after her hot and dusty walk.

At first she amused herself looking at the pictures which adorned the walls of the room; these pictures were illustrative of the lives of various saints, amongst which that of St. Anne, the patroness of the convent, figured conspicuously. They were not very interesting to Suzanne, and she therefore soon wearied of this, and sat down to think of other things more congenial to her years. She could scarcely refrain from smiling, when she imagined what her father would say, when she told him of her visit to the convent; it was such an extra-ordinary occurrence in the life of a Huguenot child.

So occupied was she with her thoughts, that the time passed unobserved, until the shades of evening began to gather, and to cast a gloom on the otherwise pleasant apartment.

A vague feeling of dread arose in the heart of Suzanne; but, as we have said before, she was a fearless child, and singularly patient. She determined, therefore, to wait, for, as she argued with herself, 'the Messieurs Prêtres are perhaps very busy; more so than they expected to be. '

At length, however, her uneasiness became so great, that she resolved to go in search of those who had brought her there; but, as might have been expected, the door was locked from the outside. The poor little girl, after vainly trying to open it, was on the point of crying out with terror, when she heard footsteps in the corridor, the key was turned in the lock, and the same lady entered, who had received her when she came with the priests.

Eagerly Suzanne questioned the Supérieure as to where they were. She for some time evaded giving a direct answer, but at last yielded to the child's pertinacity, and told her that they had been called away suddenly, and, actuated by a feeling of compassion for the poor little girl, she added, that doubtless, they would come back for here ere long, and in the meantime she would send for some refreshment, and Suzanne must try to be patient until their return.

For some moments Suzanne seemed stunned by what she heard; then the conviction forced itself upon her, that she was a prisoner. A burst of childish grief and fear overcame her, and she wept uncontrollably. The Supérieure tried all in her power to soothe her, and succeeded after a time in doing so.

Here we must leave Suzanne for the present, and return to her sorrowing parents.

THE SEARCH BEGINS

Monsieur de l'Orme, from the time of his daughter's disappearance, had made every inquiry in his power, and searched every part of the neighbouring country, in the hope of finding her, - but in vain; the influence of the priests was so thorough, their arrangements so perfect, and the dread of them so great, that all his efforts were unavailing, and he could gain no information whatever respecting her. Day after day he renewed his search, but always with the same result, and on this particular afternoon, he returned home more dejected and despairing than ever. The disappearance of Suzanne was shrouded in mystery; and the uncertainty of her being alive or dead, preyed incessantly on her father's mind.

When his wife had controlled her emotion, he told her how unsuccessful he had been, and then, with a great effort, he added, 'Madeleine, there is another trial which we must endure. '

Madame de l'Orme raised her eyes, with a mute, questioning look, and he proceeded to tell her that certain information had reached the Huguenots, that an order had gone forth from the king, commanding his Protestant subjects to abjure their faith at once; those who refused compliance were to have their houses and lands confiscated, to be thrown into prison, and if they still continued obstinate, death by torture, or on the scaffold, would in all probability be their portion. His own name, as a person of influence in the district where he dwelt, headed the list of 'postscripts;' and nothing remained for them but immediate flight.

Madeleine de l'Orme listened to her husband in profound silence. She was deadly pale, but she did not shed a tear; and when he had done speaking, she said, 'Pierre, I am ready! When do you wish us to leave?'

'This very night! It might be too late tomorrow. Our good pastor, Monsieur Morin, strongly urges our immediate departure, and I have made arrangements with our friends at Paimbœf to receive us . This day I have received a letter, telling me that the boat is in readiness to take us on board a small vessel, the captain of which is able and willing to convey us to England, where I have determined to fix our residence. He is taking in his cargo, but will so manage as to leave immediately on our arrival. I have not told you this before, and I did not wish to add to your distress and anxiety; but now, the time for action has arrived, and, as I said before, we have not a moment to lose. For the sake of our other children, it is clearly our duty to leave our native land. Madeleine, let us have our evening meal as soon as may be, that the poor little ones may go to rest early; they will have much fatigue to undergo ere we reach our destination. Shall I summon Marthe to prepare the supper, whilst we collect what we shall want for the journey?'

Madame de l'Orme assented, and sadly the husband and wife put together their valuables, and what money they had in the house; and packed up a few articles of clothing, which were indispensable, and easily carried. Whilst they pursued their melancholy task, the name of Suzanne never once passed the lips of either her father or mother, and yet their lost child was never one moment absent from the thoughts of either. Each, however, felt the necessity of concealing their grief, for the sake of the other, and they knew, too, that they must save their strength for the arduous journey which was before them.

Their old and valued servant Marthe Poirier, who had lived in the de l'Orme family from her youth, and who looked upon her master as her special property, having had the care of him in his childhood, had now to be told of their intended flight. Accordingly, Pierre and Madeleine came down to apprise her of it. They would much have wished to take her with them, but feared the old woman would never consent to leave her beloved France. In this, however, they were mistaken, for she no sooner understood the case, than she expressed her determination to follow them wherever they went, and her master and mistress gladly acquiesced. They cautioned her, however, to keep the matter a profound secret; as, were their plans to become known, the arrest of Monsieur de l'Orme would be the consequence, and destruction to himself and his family inevitable.

Marthe promised obedience to their wishes, and as soon as the meal was over, carried off the children to bed, where they were soon reposing in profound slumber.

Monsieur and Madame de l'Orme then sat down for a few brief moments to make their plans for the journey: but in a short time a low tap at the door, which opened immediately afterwards, made them both look up, and they beheld, standing in the doorway, their venerable pastor. 'Peace be to this house!' he uttered, as he came forward to greet his friends, in the affectionate manner he always used, when speaking to any member of his flock.

Monsieur Morin had numbered some seventy years. His hair was white as snow, but although an aged man, his tall, erect figure was still unbent, and the fire of his piercing eye unquenched. He had suffered much during the persecution, but, nothing daunted, he had remained unflinchingly doing his Master's work: always ready with advice or rebuke, as occasion required; and never had any one asked in vain for his help or sympathy. He was an eloquent preacher, and when he appealed to the conscience of his hearers, or poured consolation into the hearts of the afflicted, it was impossible to hear him unmoved.

He had now come to take leave of the de l'Ormes, and to express his sympathy in their misfortunes. He told them how much he approved of their determination to leave France, and when they urged him to accompany them, he replied, 'No, my friends, I cannot desert my flock in the hour of danger. I have no ties like you to bind me to this world. If it should please God to shorten my span of life, let me be found fighting at my post. 'Then rising up, he said, 'I must not detain you any longer, for doubtless you have much to do and to think of. Farewell, beloved friends! Take the blessing of an old man with you, and may He, who overrules all for our good, watch over and protect you now and ever-more!' In another moment he was gone, and Pierre and Madeleine de l'Orme, their eyes suffused with tears, saw him depart, with the conviction that they would never more meet on earth.

They now snatched a few moments repose; but a little before midnight, they were up again, finishing all their preparations.

As we have before remarked, the house in which Monsieur de l'Orme lived, was in the outskirts of the village, and detached from other habitations. At the back of it was a small courtyard, and beyond again a walled garden of considerable extent, at the end of which was a door, opening on a piece of waste land or common, which separated the garden from a small river, one of the tributary streams of the Loire.

Very lovely was that little river! In some places it was so narrow as scarcely to deserve the name, whilst in others, and particularly at the spot near which stood Monsieur de l'Orme's property, it expanded into a really respectable stream. The opposite bank was shaded by tall trees, which were reflected in the still waters beneath, and their luxuriant foliage afforded shelter to numerous shrubs and plants which grew there in picturesque confusion; while from the bosom of the limpid stream sprang a multitude of aquatic plants, each more beautiful than its neighbour. Reeds and bulrushes waved their pliant stems in the rustling breeze, and the graceful water-lily, floating on the surface of the peaceful river, pillowed its blossoms of silver and gold on a bed of emerald leaves. Here, in this enchanting spot, Madame de l'Orme had spent many pleasant hours surrounded by her children. A cluster of tall trees, with wide spreading branches, grew at a convenient distance from the house, and thither she would bring her work during the pleasant summer afternoons. Whilst thus occupied, she could watch the innocent gambols of her children: the little ones amusing themselves by gathering the daisies and butter-cups which grew profusely on the short green turf which sloped down to the water's edge; and watching the fairy circles made by the numerous denizens of the stream, as they sported hither and thither, enjoying the sunshine, and entrapping the unwary insects which skimmed along its glassy surface. Suzanne, the lost and loved Suzanne, sat by her mother's side on these occasions, sometimes engaged on some piece of work under her mother's supervision. She was a staid and sedate little maiden, but she was nevertheless often beguiled from her task by the pleading looks and coaxing tones of her little brothers and sisters, and obtaining permission, she would join in their games as merrily as the youngest amongst them. Monsieur de l'Orme often joined the happy party too, bringing his book with him; but it was generally laid aside, and his usual gravity along with it, when he heard the shouts and laughter of his little ones. Truly their mirth was contagious, and the grave Huguenot could not help joining in their harmless amusements, and relaxing the almost austere manner, which, in reality, was more habitual than natural to him. As the clock struck four, old Marthe would come out of the house laden with a basket containing the afternoon collation; soon its contents brought the hungry little troop round the presiding genius of the feast; slices of bread, and tempting fruit, were then distributed among them, together with refreshing draughts of delicious milk; and a blessing having been asked on the food they were about to partake of, the happy children and their parents eat their simple meal in thankfulness.

Such was the custom of those times, a very pleasant custom too; and such it is still in most parts of France. When it is at all possible, the higher as well as the lower classes among the French take their meals out of doors; they prefer the open air to the closeness of their houses, and with the exception of those who live in towns, and cannot of course enjoy themselves in this manner, they take advantage of any spot affording the shelter of a few trees, and there congregate to take one or another of their repasts.

Thus it was with Monsieur de l'Orme's family; and every fine day the well-ordered little flock might be found in its accustomed and favourite haunt. This beloved spot, with all its endearing associations, must now be given up, probably for ever; no wonder, then, that those among them, who were old enough to feel what they were losing, were well nigh heart-broken.

Escape in the Night

The half-hour had just chimed from the neighbouring church tower, when a small party might have been seen issuing from the garden door at the back of Monsieur de l'Orme's house, and two horses were brought out, one ready saddled, on which Madame de l'Orme was soon seated; her baby, her precious little Madeleine, was cradled in her arms. The other horse was then got ready to receive his burden; a large pannier being fastened on either side of the saddle, in which, supported by cushions, and well covered up, were placed the two other little ones, Gaston and Marie, both fast asleep. Old Marthe occupied the place between them; Jean the eldest, an intelligent boy of eleven, had the charge of leading him; whilst his father undertook the care of the one on which his wife was seated.

When all was ready, the door was locked. The agony of Madeleine de l'Orme can scarcely be imagined, much less described. For her husband's sake she tried to hide her suffering, and she partly succeeded; but at the last moment her fortitude gave way, and the cry of, 'My child! My child! My lost Suzanne! Must I leave thee?' was only hushed by the fear of endangering the lives of her other loved ones.

With many tears the little party left their beloved home, and in a sorrowful silence proceeded on their way.

Jean de l'Orme had been told of the danger they incurred of being overtaken and arrested; and being a quick-witted little boy, and moreover trained to the most perfect obedience, he understood at once what was expected of him, and adhered strictly to the rules laid down by his father.

For some time their way was along the banks of the river. It was a bright star-light night, and the air was cool and pleasant after the heat of the day. Nothing was heard but the sound of their footsteps as they fell lightly on the turf, and not a word was spoken, except in whispers, for fear of attracting the attention of their enemies. At last the high road was gained, but being some miles away from the village, they could travel in comparative safety. That part of the country being but thinly populated, there were very few houses, and those only small farms, at a great distance from each other.

Thus they journeyed on, old Marthe insisting she should share with little Jean the task of leading the horse. The boy was thus enabled to rest many times on the road, and was thereby saved much unnecessary fatigue. Poor little lad! This was a rough beginning to his life, but he was too young to realize the dangers which surrounded them. Instead of feeling fear, his lively and excitable disposition made him take a certain pleasure in the risks they ran, and their nocturnal expedition was rather a pleasure than otherwise to him.

There were several years between him and Gaston, another brother having occupied the place between them; but God had taken their little Pierre to himself a few years back, and having no one of his own age to play with, he learnt independence and self-reliance much sooner than he otherwise would have done.

Long and weary was the journey; but on the morning of the fourth day, just as the dawn was breaking, they arrived at the place of 'rendezvous. 'They could see nothing distinctly, but they heard the low murmur of the waves as they slowly dashed along the shore; and as the sound fell with a soothing influence on the ear, it seemed to whisper that deliverance was at hand, and danger over.

Monsieur de l'Orme gave a low whistle as they stopped at the edge of a small coppice by the road side. Immediately an answering note was given, and two men emerged from the shelter of the trees and bushes, greeting their friends in the warmest manner.

Paul and Victor le Grand were brothers; they were well educated for their station, and although not belonging to the same grade of society as Monsieur de l'Orme, he looked upon them as friends, and had a sincere regard for them. They were thoroughly honest, true-hearted men, men who were always ready and willing to peril life and liberty, as they were doing now, to serve a friends; aye, and a foe also, if an opportunity occurred.

They were small farmers, who cultivated with their own hands the inheritance left to them by their father. Being thrifty and frugal in their manner of living, they had saved up a considerable sum of money; and, at the time of which we write, were part-owners of the vessel which was to convey the exiles to the shores of England. The produce of their land was carried to the neighbouring sea-port, where it found a ready sale, being shipped at once for other lands.

Their abode was a substantial cottage or farm-house, built of stone, which looked as if it had endured many a fierce ocean blast, and would endure many more. It was a long low building, with a mountain of thatch for a roof, and it had small latticed windows, protected at night by heavy wooden shutters, which effectually resisted the storms and tempests of the winter months. Altogether it was a most comfortable dwelling, and to its shelter they now prepared to conduct the weary fugitives.

The day had now fully dawned; and as they traversed the short distance which separated them from the le Grands' dwelling, the travellers saw much to wonder at and admire, for none of the party (with the exception of Monsieur de l'Orme, who had frequently visited his friends) had ever seen the sea before. A long line of low sandy beach extended for miles along the shore, and was terminated by a bold headland at one extremity, whilst a corresponding mass of rock at the other end of the bay completely hid from view the neighbouring town, which was only a few miles distant from this spot. Lovely, most lovely, was the scene on which they gazed; the tide was coming up, and as the sun rose in all his splendour, the little waves, as they danced along the shore, looked as if they were crested with gold and gems. It was a perfect calm; earth, sea and sky seemed enjoying a sort of charmed repose, most soothing to the sorrowing hearts of the poor bereaved parents, who appeared to derive consolation and peace from the scene around them.

The cottage was soon reached; and at the door standing to receive them, was a middle-aged, kindly-looking woman, a step-sister of the le Grands, who, from their childhood, had looked after her brothers, their mother having died a few months after the birth of Victor.

Jeanne le Grand welcomed her guests with a grace and cordiality scarcely to be expected from one in her station. She ushered them into the only sitting-room, which was actually nothing more than a large well-kept kitchen; they were soon divested of their encumbering wraps, and the children, having had their hunger appeased, were carried off by Marthe to enjoy the repose they so much needed after their long journey. Their mother was glad to follow their example; and at the invitation of Jeanne, she too was soon installed in her own little room, where she fell into a deep, dreamless slumber.

Monsieur de l'Orme remained below with Paul le Grand,

making plans for the future, and consulting with him, as to the best means of carrying on a correspondence without fear of detection. He was naturally anxious to hear if any tidings should be obtained of his unfortunate Suzanne, as Monsieur Morin had promised to let the le Grands know if he received any information respecting her. Upwards of an hour passed thus; and having made all their arrangements, they were quite ready to receive Victor, who now returned with the intelligence that the boat was waiting for them, and the vessel coming round the point.

All was now hurry and confusion; the children and Madame de l'Orme were aroused from their slumbers, and soon fully equipped for the long voyage before them. The view which greeted their sight, as they emerged from the cottage, was indeed a glorious one. The sea was very calm, and reflected the glistening sails of many a fishing-boat, which had left the shore whilst the travellers were enjoying their short repose. Numbers of people, living in the neighbouring huts and cottages, were on the beach collecting sea-weed, which had been washed up by the tide. The sea-weed is invaluable to the farmer, as well as to the poor cottager, who trust to it for fuel during the greater part of the year. As the waves deposit it on the beach, men, women, and even children are ready to draw it up with long rakes on the sand or shingle; when they have collected as much as they can, they spread it out, and they may be seen turning it over and over until it is perfectly dry. When this process is over, the women wheel it up in barrows to a convenient place near the house or cottage, and there it is piled up in huge stacks ready for use. It makes a capital fire, and the ashes are used for manure, as well as the sea-weed itself before it is dried. When it is in that state, it is spread over the ground, and is supposed to contribute much to its fertility. The picturesque costume of the sea-weed gatherers, together with their occupation, attracted at once the attention of the children, who had never witnessed anything like it before; and Marthe was plied with questions, which she often found difficult to answer, but they served to divert the poor old woman's thoughts, and her sorrows at leaving her native land was lessened, by having no leisure to dwell on it.

Not so Monsieur and Madame de l'Orme; when the moment for parting actually arrived, their hearts were torn with anguish. The thought of their lost child was incessantly present to their minds; and although they inwardly prayed for strength to bear the trial which God had sent them, the struggle for composure was a fearful one. Their friends accompanied them to the water's edge, where, to a rude landing place composed of rough stones piled one above another for the convenience of the fishermen, the boat was moored. There they took leave of Jeanne le Grand, her brothers only accompanying them to the vessel. At last, all are settled in their places, the rope is unfastened, the boat is pushed off, and the oars dipped briskly in the water, sending up showers of spray, which falling again into the sea like diamonds, elicited shouts of wonder and delight from the children, who, poor little things, were quite unconscious of the ruin which had fallen on their once happy home. The last voiceless adieu was at length waved, and the exiles realized, in all its bitterness, the misery which had overtaken them. 'Adieu! France bien aimée! Adieu! Pauvre patrie!' burst from their aching hearts, as they stretched out their hands despairingly towards the receding shore; and little Jean, old enough to understand all his parents were suffering, laid his head on his mother's lap, and mingled his tears and sobs with hers.

The vessel is at last reached; and the travellers with their scanty baggage safely deposited on deck. The parting with their two devoted friends is spoken, and they are left alone. Pierre and Madeleine de l'Orme stood in silence watching the boat which conveyed the le Grand's back to their home, until it became a mere speck almost invisible to the eye. As they stood thus, Madeleine suddenly turning towards her husband, exclaimed, 'Pierre! Will you promise me one thing.'

Her face wore so hopeful an expression, that Monsieur

de l'Orme gazed at it in astonishment, as he answered, 'Most certainly! If it is in my power. '

'Will you promise, that when once we are settled in England, you will return to search for our beloved child? Oh, Pierre! My husband! I feel here (laying her hand on her heart as she spoke) that our Suzanne is still living, though hidden from our sight. God has surely sent that thought to comfort me; and, Pierre, you will grant my request, will you now?'

Pierre de l'Orme looked down fondly on the fair face of his wife, now wan and pallid with sorrow and fatigue; and although he felt almost convinced in his own mind that his child had ceased to exist, he had not the courage to take the mother's hope away from her. He, however, was aware of the risk he would run in returning to France; and although he had no fears for himself personally, yet he knew how dependent on his exertions his family would be, that the very subsistence of his wife and young children must be gained by (most probably) the labour of his hands, and he was reluctant to promise what poor Madeleine so earnestly pleaded for.

She saw his hesitation, and divining the cause, she said, 'Pierre, I know what you are thinking of; but, my husband, God will take care of us! Has He not already preserved us from innumerable dangers? Has he not been to us, as to the Israelites of old, "a pillar of fire by night, and a pillar of cloud by day?" Oh, Pierre! Yes, the moon and the stars lighted us on our perilous journey hither during the hours of darkness, and He must have spread an invisible cloud around our path by day, for did we not pass every where unquestioned and unscathed?'

'Madeleine! I stand rebuked! I promise, and may God forgive my want of faith!'

He then proceeded to give his wife an account of the conversation he had had with Paul le Grand, and the arrangements they had made with regard to the future. The day thus passed slowly away; towards evening a light breeze having sprung up in their favour, they made more progress than they had yet done.

Their voyage was necessarily a long one. In those days vessels were not built as they are now, and they were clumsy things at the best; but they had a kind captain and a steady crew, and they were content to abide patiently until it should please God to bring them to the end of their journey. The children were full of excitement at the novelty of every thing around them, and kept poor old Marthe perpetually on the alert to prevent their getting into mischief.

At length the voyage was accomplished, they were landed on the shores of England, and proceeded at once to London. They had brought letters of introduction to other refugees, who, like themselves, had been obliged to fly from their native land; and these, having been sometimes settled in the country, had acquired some knowledge of the language, and were thus enabled to help the poor strangers.

Through the kind exertions of their new friends, they found a lodging suitable to their small means; and Monsieur de l'Orme soon obtained employment as teacher of languages in schools and private families. His grave, gentlemanly manners won respect from everybody, and he had as much occupation as he could manage. This was far better than he had expected, and it gave him hope that a brighter future was in store for himself and his family.

Having now seen the exiles safely settled in their new home, it is time to return to our little heroine.

THE LITTLE PRISONER

We left Suzanne de l'Orme in the convent parlour, waiting patiently for the re-appearance of her supposed protectors; but she waited in vain. In answer to a wish she expressed of being allowed to return home, although night had already set in, she was told it would not be prudent for her to do so, neither was it possible to send any one with her. She was overwhelmed with grief at this announcement, and wept as if her heart would break. The Supérieure, a good kind-hearted woman, was really grieved at her distress; she reasoned with the child, and made use of every argument she could think of to allay her fears; but for a time she was perfectly unsuccessful.

At length Suzanne became more calm. She remembered that God was watching over her, and would permit no evil to befall her, if she trusted in Him. This thought brought peace and hope to her mind; and in her own simple way, she prayed mentally for divine protection, and assuredly her prayer was heard.

Seeing her more composed, the Lady Abbess thought it best to send her to rest at once; and having rung the bell, gave orders to the sister who answered the summons, to have a little bed prepared in her own dormitory for the child.

When all was ready, the little prisoner (for such she was) was conducted to her pallet; and quite worn out with the unusual excitement and distress she had undergone, was ere long enjoying the repose she so much needed.

The next morning, however, fresh difficulties arose, and the poor little girl then became perfectly aware that she was caught in a trap, from which no exertions of her own could set her free. She therefore resolved to wait patiently until deliverance came; and from that moment never doubted that it would come soon or late. The Supérieure, notwithstanding the errors of her creed, was a truly conscientious woman. She had been induced to co-operate with the priests in their endeavour to make a convert of Suzanne de l'Orme; and she thought that by so doing she was serving God.

When she promised her help, she had no idea of what their plans were; and it is but justice to say, that even now, at this early stage of the proceedings, she was ashamed and disgusted by the deception which had been practised on the child; and she determined that her detention should be made as pleasant as possible whilst she remained under her roof. As Abbess of St. Anne's, she possessed a certain amount of power, which even the priests could not trench upon, and she was resolved to exercise that power. True to her faith, she was willing to do everything she could to convert the child from the errors in which she sincerely believed her to have been reared; but she was too noble to lend herself to anything that was not strictly honourable, and she made up her mind to find out what was really expected of her, before binding herself to any act which she should hereafter be sorry for.

When therefore Father Anselmo, the spiritual adviser of the establishment, made his appearance the following morning, accompanied by the elder of the two priests who had brought little Suzanne to the convent, she at once asked what they intended to do. Her manner was so dignified and her tone so decided, that the ecclesiastics immediately saw she would brook no control in the house where she ruled, and they thought it better to dissemble for the present.

Their intention was, if possible, by fair means, to win little Suzanne to renounce the Protestant faith; but if kindness failed, severity, and even force, would be employed to attain their end.

This latter alternative they did not, however, impart to the Supérieure, feeling sure she would never countenance anything of the kind; it would therefore be necessary to remove the little girl entirely from the convent, if the latter plan had to be adopted. They did not, however, anticipate much trouble from so young a child, and accordingly begged that Suzanne might have every indulgence – toys and sweetmeats were to be given to her – and she was to be tempted by the promise of fine dresses and a speedy return to her home, as soon as she complied with their wishes. In the meantime the Supérieure was requested to attend to the religious instruction of the child, assisted by the most zealous of the sisterhood; and the father confessor was to come himself every day to see what progress she made.

Poor Suzanne was at first very wretched notwithstanding her many indulgences; but a little by degrees she became reconciled to her lot. She was so young and so hopeful, that although she never for one moment forgot her home or her family, she could not help enjoying the little pleasures which were daily provided for her.

Her great trouble was when the priests paid their periodical visit, and puzzled her mind with questions which she often found impossible to answer. The Supérieure was always present at those interviews, and by her gentleness reassured the poor-bewildered child, when her tormentors pressed her too hard.

This went on for some weeks; but the priests made no progress whatever with the little Huguenot, who invariably replied to their exhortations, 'My father and mother never taught me such things, and I am sure it cannot be right. I wish to remain a Protestant, and go back to my dear home. '

The patience of the two men was by this time exhausted; speaking to her roughly, they told her she never should see her parents again; that she was an obstinate little heretic, who would be compelled to renounce her faith whether she liked it or not. Poor Suzanne was very much terrified, and appealed to the Supérieure for protection from their violence.

The good woman soothed her as much as she could; but, at the same time, she tried to persuade her to do as the priests wished, and added, she very much feared that what they had told her was true, and that she never would see her parents more, for intelligence had reached the convent that they had fled from their country never to return. If Suzanne would only adopt the Romish faith instead of her own, she would gladly receive her into the convent, and replace as much as she could the mother she had lost.

The child was speechless with amazement for some moments after hearing this, but an observation from one of the priests recalled her to herself. He insinuated that since her parents had deserted her, she no longer owed them obedience; and that she ought to listen to the advice of those who were willing to protect her.

'Do you mean to say,' she replied, 'that because my dear parents have been obliged to go away from this place, I am no longer to remember their wishes, and that I am to forget all their kindness to me? I cannot think so, and even if it were true – which it is not – I still owe obedience to God; He would be angry with me if I did as you bid me, for He says, we must honour and obey our parents, - this is one of His commandments, - and would punish me, if I were weak enough to believe what you say:' then turning to the Supérieure with tears in her eyes, she exclaimed, 'Ah, madame! It may be true that I shall never see my dear father and mother, and brothers and sisters any more on earth; but you surely would not wish to deprive me of the hope of meeting them all in heaven?'

The Supérieure was deeply moved, and drawing the little one towards her, endeavoured to console her, telling her she should have time to reflect on the offer which had been made, and she hoped Suzanne was convinced, that what she urged was for her good, both here and hereafter.

The child was then dismissed, and the priests having consulted together in a low voice, Father Anselmo announced his determination to take her away from the Supérieure's gentle influence; that he had orders from those high in authority to remove her, and to place her under stricter rule; and he concluded by saying, she must be in readiness to leave the following evening.

The Supérieure remonstrated – but in vain; Father Anselmo was determined, and a sinister smile crossed his countenance, as he thought he would soon have unlimited control over the helpless child. She saw that smile, and drawing herself up to her full height, she exclaimed, in a voice full of dignity, 'Very well! It shall be as you desire, and I shall be in readiness to accompany her wherever it will be your pleasure to take her. '

'There will be no necessity for you to take so much trouble, I shall go myself with the little heretic, and that will be sufficient protection!'

'Pardon me, Father Anselmo, the child was placed under my care, and I shall not leave her until I see her safe in some convent; she is too young to travel with strangers. I have permission from the Lord Bishop of this province to leave my house when necessity calls me to do so, and I shall now avail myself of that permission. I wish you good morning. 'With these words she swept majestically out of the room, apparently unconcerned – but in her own mind convinced – that she had that day made an enemy who would never desist till he had brought about her ruin. She was a courageous woman, however, and she resolved to do her duty, come what might.

We must now say a few words about Father Anselmo, as he plays a conspicuous part in the events we are now describing. He was Italian by birth, but the greater part of his life had been passed in France, and he spoke the language fluently. His age was about fifty – his stature about the middle height – and his countenance one not easily forgotten. His features had the regularity common to his countrymen, and although he could, when it so pleased him, make himself most agreeable, he was, generally quite the reverse. His complexion was olive, without a particle of colouring to relieve its almost deathlike hue; and a quantity of jet black hair, plentifully sprinkled with grey, overshadowing a low mean forehead, added to his unprepossessing appearance; whilst a pair of small piercing black eyes gleamed from under large shaggy eyebrows, the same colour as his hair. His character was crafty and cruel; and to gain his ends, he was perfectly unscrupulous as to the means he employed. Into the hands of this man our poor little Suzanne had fallen, and nothing but the interposition of providence could save her.

The Supérieure too, felt the weight of his displeasure from the moment she attempted to thwart his designs; and when he, a few years afterwards, joined a band of renegade priests, who abjured their religion and denied their God, he denounced the unhappy lady as one who was an enemy to her country, and she fell a victim to the revenge of that bad man. She was dragged from her beloved home, and after much suffering and persecution, death put an end to her miseries.

This is a digression, but it is necessary to the proper understanding of the story. The following evening, as Father Anselmo had announced, he was at the convent gate with a clumsy sort of vehicle, such as was in use at the time of which we write. Into this vehicle the Supérieure and her little charge were placed, Father Anselmo seated himself opposite to them, and the journey commenced. As may be supposed, there was very little conversation between the priest and his elder companion; they were both occupied with their own thoughts, which they were careful not to communicate to each other. As to little Suzanne, she was too sad to think of anything but of her parents; and she also felt she could not speak on the subject nearest to her heart in the presence of the man, who seemed to exercise too terrible an influence on her destiny.

Thus they journeyed on, only stopping to change horses, and to get the food necessary for themselves. During the day the elders of the party studied their breviaries, and appeared completely absorbed in their devotions. Occasionally the priest would raise his eyes, and fix them with a peculiar expression on his companions; this was unnoticed except by Suzanne, who shuddered as she observed his look, although she hardly knew why she did so.

At length, after many weary days of travelling, they reached Paris, and their conductor stopped his vehicle before a large gloomy looking building, in a narrow un-frequented street. The bell was rung, and the portress having opened the gate, the whole party drove into the court-yard, where, having alighted, they were ushered into a scantily furnished apartment, very different from the pleasant parlour at St. Anne's. In a few moments, a woman who announced herself as the head of the establishment, came in, and into her hands the priest, with an ill-concealed air of triumph, committed little Suzanne. The good Supérieure's heart sank within her, when she saw what sort of a person was to have the care of the hapless little girl. She was a coarse, vulgar woman, who had been raised to the station she occupied, by those who wanted an unscrupulous person as their tool, and they could not have made a better selection – for La Mere Monique, as she was called, never had any qualms of conscience, and acted up to the orders given to her without question or comment.

The Supérieure saw at a glance what poor little Suzanne's future lot was to be; but although her heart bled at the thought of what the child would have to endure, she repressed all outward expression of her feelings, wisely supposing that any expostulation on her part would only increase the poor little one's sufferings. Seeing, therefore, that her presence was no longer desired, she took an affectionate leave of the unfortunate child, and imploring fervently God's blessing on her, she went her way, merely commending her to the kindness of her new protectress. Alas! Her wildest imaginings fell far short of what the poor child had eventually to undergo.

TRIALS AND ENDEAVOURS

No sooner had the door closed on her kind friend, than Suzanne was roughly told she must *now* obey, or the severest measures would be adopted to make her do so. The priest and his ally spoke in loud threatening tones, and when the child made no answer, they shook her violently. It was in vain, however; Suzanne was past hearing or comprehension; faint and exhausted after a long journey, she stared vacantly at them, trying to take in their meaning; but they soon saw she was incapable of understanding what they told her. La Mere Monique had still some remnant of womanly feeling in her nature, and she suggested it would be better to let her have a night's rest and some food before proceeding to extremities. The priest assented, being tired himself; and poor little Suzanne was carried off by her new guardian to the refectory, where something in the shape of a meal was set before her. For sometime she refused to eat – indeed she was almost incapable of doing so; fearing that the child would fall ill – a thing she by no means desired – the woman insisted on her swallowing some wine and eating a little bread; after which she was carried off to bed, where she sobbed herself to sleep, after commending herself to the care of her heavenly Father.

The next morning another trial of her constancy was made; failing in their endeavours, her tormentors began a series of persecutions, which seem incredible in our times. She was beaten – half-starved – and kept in solitary confinement in one of the dark underground cells of the establishment. These punishments were mild compared with others to which she was subjected. Father Anselmo was an adept in all things which could give pain; and his instructions were given that every refinement of cruelty should be employed, so as to extort a confession from the wretched child, that the Romish Faith was the only one by which her soul could be saved. Hunger and bodily, pain, sickness or fear could not however shake her steadfast belief in her creed and in her God; she had help from above to withstand temptation, and she baffled her persecutors. Father Anselmo had been in foreign lands and among savage tribes, whom, in the earlier part of his life he had endeavoured to rescue from heathenism; he had himself suffered persecution and torture, barely escaping with life. This treatment, instead of softening, had hardened his heart, which was naturally prone to cruelty; having no truly religious feeling or love for his Saviour, he, in the proud boastfulness of his nature, thought that he would exercise the power he possessed, so as to coerce those unfortunates who had the temerity to hold different views to his. He therefore adopted the mode of treatment he had received at the hands of the savages, to gain his own ends, and not only Suzanne de l'Orme, but numbers of hapless Huguenots suffered unheard of cruelties by his orders and under his superintendence. Poor Suzanne's fragile frame was little fitted for the hardships and bad treatment she was exposed to; in addition to what has been said, she was often fastened tightly, for hours together, in a constrained position, to a stake securely fixed in the ground; her limbs cramped from inaction, became powerless when released, and she was left alone to recover as best she might. Fainting at times from fatigue and exhaustion, cold water was dashed in her face, and she would return to consciousness, only to deplore that it had not pleased God to take her to himself, and end her misery. At other times, her usual fare of coarse black bread and water, was varied by still coarser food, which at times was so loathsome that she could not swallow it, and on these occasions she was left until the following day, without even a morsel to appease the hunger which tormented her. At intervals her rest was broken by sounds calculated to frighten a child of her years; and then she would awake in the wildest terror, shaking in every limb, and afraid to go to sleep again for fear of the same terrible interruption to her slumbers. The unfortunate child was only released from confinement at stated intervals to go and listen to the services of the Church of Tome in the convent chapel, after which she was re-conducted to her prison, and left alone for the time with her thoughts. Alone! Oh, no! God's angels surely watched over her, and prevented her from giving way to utter despondency.

When in the solitude of her cell, she lay on the bundle of straw which was called her bed. She whiled away the time by repeating the hymns and prayers she had been taught in her dear home, and by recalling the stories she had heard of martyred children; and she prayed, if such should be her destiny, that God would give her strength to suffer and endure as they did. Time wore on, winter approached, and often the poor shivering child was half frozen in her cell. She walked to and fro to keep up the circulation in her veins; and so wearisome was the life she led, that she even began to look forward to the hour when she should be summoned to the chapel – for it was a break in the monotony of her existence. She never, however, for one moment joined in the services, or allowed herself to be unfaithful to the creed in which she had been brought up.

Father Anselmo, after a few days sojourn in Paris, had been obliged to return to Saumur; but he made arrangements to come periodically and look after his little prisoner. He accordingly returned about two months afterwards, and was so little satisfied with the progress made towards her conversion, that he determined to take her back with him, so that she might be under his more immediate superintendence. La Mere Monique, who was well paid for the work she had undertaken, endeavoured to combat his resolution, but he only sneered at her arguments, and told her to have the child in readiness to depart at a moment's notice. She dared not disobey; and poor Suzanne's preparations did not require much time or trouble. When the sister, who had brought her meals, told Suzanne the following evening that Father Anselmo was coming to fetch her early the next day, she gave a little start of pleasure. She thought he was going to take her back to the good Supérieure; and much as she disliked the man, she felt almost impatient for the moment of his arrival. The poor child little knew how far such a thought was from his mind. He had not the slightest intention of taking her to St. Anne's; but his plan was to have her in the neighbourhood, see her when he pleased, and break (what he called) her stubborn will.

The next day he came for the child. They journeyed back much in the same way that they had come, except only that Suzanne missed the gentle companionship of her friend the Supérieure, more than she could have thought possible; for she had learnt to love her, and now looked forward to the meeting with her, as if she had been a near relative.

At last their conveyance stopped near a low mean-looking house some leagues from Saumur; and Father Anselmo having alighted, he commanded Suzanne to do the same. No one noticing their arrival, he shouted, 'Hola! Is there no one at home?' At the same time giving a vigorous rap on the half-open door. An old woman at last made her appearance, and recognizing the priest, apologized humbly for having kept him waiting; but he cut her short, and bade her call her husband.

She soon returned with him; and Father Anselmo turning to the man, said 'Simon! Here is the girl I have spoken to you about; are you willing to take her on my terms?'

Etienne Simon (for such was his name) looked at her from head to foot, then said in a sulky manner, 'She does not seem fit for much.'

'Fit or not, will you undertake her; that is the question? You may do what you like with her – the obstinate little heretic – make her your servant, or, if you like it better, teach her to make bricks,' and he laughed derisively; 'I'll warrant Mademoiselle will soon tire of this, and will then be glad enough to give up her absurd notions; we shall find her tractable enough after a week or two of your tender mercies. Allons; is it a bargain?'

'As you will,' replied the other; 'a bargain is a bargain, but I have no doubt I shall find the girl more plague than profit! I promise you, however, she will have no time for laziness, so you may rely on me.'

Suzanne heard all like one in a dream. She looked from one to the other, as if asking for an explanation; but finding that no one noticed her, she asked the priest in a timid trembling voice, what it all meant?

'It means,' he replied, 'that since you are so obstinate, you shall be compelled to obey. Now we shall see what hard work will do; and I can tell you, you will not be spared. Maître Etienne is not over tender, and he has my leave to beat you as much as he likes, whenever you disobey his orders. I would advise you, therefore, for your own sake, to be more tractable than you have hitherto been.'

'Oh, Monsieur! You cannot mean to leave me here with these people? Oh, pray, pray, take me away.'

'Will you renounce your faith, and become a member of the only true Church, if I grant your wish?'

Suzanne was sorely tempted, and for one moment she hesitated – the next, a vision of her happy home, and her beloved parents, floated before her, and some unseen voice seemed to whisper, 'Be steadfast!' She raised her head and said firmly, but respectfully, 'I cannot do so, Monsieur; it would be wicked, and God would punish me for it; oh, do not ask me!' she added, in a tone of entreaty.

Father Anselmo gave her a look of inconceivable hatred; and in a tone almost inarticulate with rage, he replied, 'then you shall stay here until you submit!' and turning to Simon, he exclaimed, 'look here, fellow; I command you not to spare her; I shall be responsible for anything you may do to her, and I have full authority for what I do. Do you hear?'

'Yes!' replied Simon, sulkily; 'you need not fear my being over-indulgent. '

'Well! If you obey my orders, you shall not be the loser,' was the reply of the cruel man; and turning to leave the house, he encountered the gaze of his little victim. The wretched child looked at fixedly – her agony was too great even for tears; but in a broken and husky voice, she said, 'God forgive you for your cruelty to one who has never harmed you!' With these words she turned away and covered her face with her hands, whilst a mute supplication for help went up from her heart to her Father in heaven. When she looked up again the priest was gone!

A New Abode

The departure of Father Anselmo was a relief to Suzanne, for his presence inspired her with unaccountable dread. She seemed to feel instinctively that she was an object of antipathy to him – nay, almost of abhorrence. Her feeling on the subject was a correct one; for her steadfast opposition to all his schemes for her conversion, had roused the evil passions in that bad man's nature; and his proud spirit was galled beyond control at being thwarted by one, whom he had deemed too young and insignificant even to have an opinion of her own; much less to withstand the force of his arguments, or attempt to go against his will. Great was his wrath, therefore, at the discovery which he made, and he was at no pains to hide his dislike to his poor little victim. Suzanne therefore felt some degree of relief at his departure; and old Simon having left the house at the same time as the priest, she ventured to survey her future home.

The room she was in was a sort of kitchen with an earthen floor, rough and uneven, and indescribably dirty; bones, cabbage-stalks, and the relics of many a meal being strewed about in every direction. Fowls were strutting about picking up what suited them best, whilst a couple of dogs were snarling and fighting over some dainty morsel which each coveted. An old rickety table, and one or two wooden benches, constituted the furniture, whilst large cupboards, inserted in the walls, contained beds for the inmates of the establishment. A curtain of red and white checked cotton hung loosely across the window, a very insufficient protection from the cold blast, which entered through every chink and crevice. The only other room in that house was also on the ground floor, and there was a door of communication between the two. This latter room was only used as a receptacle for lumber, and as the sleeping apartment of the domestic animals.

Having taken in all these details at a glance, Suzanne's eyes next rested on the woman, who had received them on their arrival.

She was seated near the large hearth preparing some vegetables for the mid-day meal; and as she finished each portion, she threw it into the 'Marmite,' which was suspended over the wood fire in the huge fire-place. She was a small woman, with a complexion tanned by constant exposure to the sun, until it had become like that of a gypsy. Her face was wrinkled, and her eyes dark and piercing; but Suzanne thought she saw a look of compassion in those eyes, and she was right. Old Margot was a woman and a mother, rude and degraded though she was; and the sight of Suzanne touched a chord in her poor withered heart, bringing to her remembrance a little child of her own, who was lying in the church-yard of the neighbouring village. A tear dimmed her eye, and she felt pity for the poor outcast.

Marguerite Simon, or as she was generally called, 'Margot,' had not always been as she then was. In her youth she was a pretty, light-hearted brunette, whose misfortune it was to be united to a coarse brutal man, who cared nothing for her, and who soon neglected her. Gradually his ill-usage had rendered her what she now was – a peevish, fretful woman, to whom a kind word was never addressed, and whose life was one endless round of misery and discomfort. She was not naturally bad-tempered, but she had been soured by constant worry and disappointment; and her once merry disposition had become chilled, and her light heart almost turned to stone, by the daily recurrence of the fearful scenes of disorder and unruly passion which she was compelled to witness without the power of preventing. In the first days of her married life, the violence of her husband terrified her almost out of her senses; but by degrees she became accustomed to his bursts of passion, and coarse abusive language, till she at last became an apathetic witness of his fury, and went about her usual occupations without seeming to notice him. There were times, however, when her spirit was roused beyond endurance, and she would hurl an angry retort at the madman whom she had the ill-fortune to call husband, and who was cowardly enough to inflict blows in return – blows so heavy as at times to fell her to the earth. With all her trouble, Marguerite Simon had brought up a large family as well as she was able; but all were married or dead with the exception of one son, who had grown up the counterpart of his father, both in character and appearance, and who assisted him not only in his daily work, but in tormenting and worrying his wretched mother.

Oh, it was a terrible household that in which Father Anselmo placed his poor victim; and, if anything could have shaken her constancy, what she heard and witnessed there, must assuredly have done so. But the crafty priest was foiled even here.

Notwithstanding all her misery, there was still some feeling left in old Margot's breast, and the sight of the poor forlorn little girl moved her strangely. It was therefore with a softer accent than usual that she addressed the child, saying, 'Are you not cold? Come hither and warm yourself!'

This act of kindness, slight though it was, touched the heart of poor Suzanne; the long pent up tears gushed from her eyes as she vainly tried to articulate her thanks, and the sobs which shook her frame were so violent, that old Margot became much alarmed. Having made her drink some water, she by a great effort calmed herself, and by degrees regained her composure. Being questioned by the old woman, Suzanne told her the sufferings she had already undergone; and knowing well from experience what she might expect at the hands of her husband and son, Marguerite Simon then and there formed the resolution to shield her as much as possible from their brutality. It was little she could do, poor creature, but that little was always some addition to the child's comfort.

The dinner was now ready, and the two men came in. Suzanne looked at them in fear and trembling, and they in return scowled at her savagely. The younger man was very tall, quite six feet high; and his unwashed face, and uncombed hair, made him look a perfect savage. The conversation between him and his father (if conversation it could be called) was garnished with oaths and foul language; such language as Suzanne de l'Orme had never heard, and happily for her, poor child, did not understand. They ate their coarse meal voraciously, throwing the refuse of their food on the floor, and drinking copious draughts of thin sour wine, which aggravated their ill-humour, and made them still more savage than before. When they had satisfied their appetite, Etienne Simon turning to her, said, 'Look sharp! Don't stay there, come into the brickfield; I'll find work for you to do, you good-for-nothing little heretic!'

Thus apostrophized, poor Suzanne again burst into tears, and the ruffian shouting out, 'Hold that noise, and do as you are bid,' was about to drag her out of the house after him, when his wife exclaimed, 'Don't you see the child is worn out with fatigue? She is not capable of doing anything to-day; let her alone till tomorrow, and I'll answer for it she will work better after a night's rest. '

With an oath and a growl he desisted; but as he reached the

door, he turned round and said, 'I'll let you off now; but mind, if you are not up at daybreak tomorrow, you'll feel the weight of my hand. Do you hear, girl?'

'Yes!' was the almost inaudible reply; and the unfeeling pair went out to their accustomed work.

Again had a woman's voice interposed between her and the cruelty of man; and little Suzanne never forgot that act of kindness. When she had recovered from the emotion which had so nearly overpowered her, she asked old Margot if she could help about her household work; but the woman replied, 'She could do very well without her assistance, she had not been accustomed to be helped.' Suzanne, however, insisted; she said 'it would do her good to be occupied about something, it would divert her thoughts and prevent her dwelling on her wretchedness;' and her willingness to be of use, and gentleness of manner, quite won the old woman's heart. As the day came to a close, Margot, fearing further violence from her husband and son, gave Suzanne a crust of bread and a little milk, advising her at the same time to go to bed. She willingly acquiesced; and, following her guide out of the house, she led her to a stable at a little distance from it. When there, Margot gave her a woollen covering of some sort, and bidding her 'good night,' told her to climb up into a loft and there, amongst the hay, to make a bed for herself; then taking away the ladder, she left the child alone, and went back to her comfortless home, wondering what strange chance had brought this new addition to her household, and inwardly hoping she would find a companion in the little girl, who for some time at least was destined to be an inmate of the house. She seemed to feel that the presence of Suzanne de l'Orme would prove a blessing to her in some shape or other, and took to her at once. It was a new era in the life of a friendless and desolate woman, who only needed some one to care for, to bring out the kindliness of heart she had once possessed, and which had been nearly extinguished by the ill-treatment and brutality of her own relatives. The miserable child excited her compassion;

and as time went on, that feeling expanded into a warmer one. To this Suzanne was indebted for the few comforts she enjoyed whilst under that roof.

Happily it was yet daylight when she went up to her dormitory, and she therefore had time to get accustomed to the place. Many a girl brought up in comfort and comparative luxury, as Suzanne de l'Orme had been, would have felt frightened at being in an out-house – at night – alone – and with no human being near her, whom she could call in case of need. They would then, without further pressing, have made up their minds to do Father Anselmo's bidding; so that by abjuring their faith, they might have at least a home amongst beings of their own station in life; where they would be spared the infliction of hearing the foul language which the taskmasters had used that day. Not so our little heroine; dreadful as her situation promised to be, she meekly accepted what God pleased to send her; and, on her knees, prayed to be enabled to withstand the trials and temptations which might be in store for her.

It may appear strange that so young a child should have had such strong religious feelings; but she seemed to have grown suddenly old, and to have lived years instead of months, since she parted with her father and mother. Moreover, we must remember, that she had been peculiarly educated. It is not, therefore very surprising that her natural thoughtfulness of character was still more strongly developed by the scenes through which she passed; and that, in the absence of all earthly comfort and consolation, she turned to the Giver of all good things, with a simple faith in His power to save her from her enemies. Poor little girl! She laid herself down and slept calmly and peacefully; for the Lord sustained her.

At dawn the following morning, she was awakened by a rough voice calling out to her; and jumping up hastily, was soon ready to go down the ladder, which had been replaced for her accommodation.

After a hasty meal, she was obliged to follow Etienne Simon

and his son into the brickfield; not to learn to make bricks – but to help to carry them when made, on a hand-barrow. To look at that poor shivering child, sinking under a load too heavy for her strength, would have melted the hardest heart; but these two men knew no pity – the little intellect they ever possessed was almost extinguished by intemperance; and when, under its influence, their evil passions were aroused to such a pitch, that they were scarcely human. Hard words and blows the poor little girl was often called upon to endure; but she meekly bore all, and tried to think of her Saviour, and of the example He has left for all to follow. The words, 'When He was reviled, He reviled not again,' were ever present to her mind, and enabled her to bear her cross in patience and lowliness. The never failing hope that God would, in His own good time, send her father thither, was constantly in her thoughts; and in this hope she lived on from day to day – without it she must have died.

A WRETCHED WINTER

We must now describe the place in which these scenes were enacted, as it will be necessary to understand the locality later.

The house, if house it could be called, in which Etienne Simon and his family lived, was situated on a large open space; the soil on which it stood being composed of clay, and adapted to the purposes of brick-making – the occupation of these people. On one side it was divided from the neighbouring fields and orchards by a narrow lane, which lane had a high hedge on either side of it. To the left of the house was a large brickfield, where Simon and his son spent most of their time, pursuing their usual avocations; and the stable, in the loft of which Suzanne de l'Orme slept, was at the back of the house, but more towards the lane than otherwise, and could be seen from it distinctly. On the hedge which separated the lane from the open ground grew a row of large oak trees, which cast a pleasant shade on the otherwise unsheltered spot; and the spaces between them were filled up with brushwood and creeping plants, which formed a sort of screen and prevented the curious wayfarer from seeing into the enclosure, unless he actually mounted the hedge for the purpose of doing so.

This portion of the field was the only redeeming feature about the place, which otherwise was barren enough; nothing being visible but long rows of bricks ready for the kiln, and heaps of material waiting to be moulded into shape. True, there was a plot of ground set apart for the growth of cabbages and other vegetables required for the use of the family; but all else was bare, with the exception of a broad strip of herbage under the trees. There was a road to the village, which was half a mile distant, but it was nothing more than a cross road, and ran on the other side of a brick-field; and as the house was quite isolated, very few people passed that way, except those who had business to transact with Simon.

The exterior of the house was not inviting; indeed it was in a very bad state of repair. The walls were roughly plastered with a sort of yellowish clay, mixed with chopped straw sticking out every here and there; the plaster was falling off in many places, leaving bare and unsightly patches of brick and stone exposed to view. A thatched roof, much dilapidated, was surmounted by a couple of rickety looking chimneys; and the dirty window panes, thick with cobwebs and dust, were many of them broken, and stuffed with rags to exclude the wind and rain.

In front of the door was a pool of stagnant water, in which dabbled a few ducks; and a lean long-legged pig roamed about the neglected yard in search of whatever food he could find. The interior we have before described, but words are wanting to give an idea of the squalor and filth of the whole establishment. It suited those who occupied it; but to a child like Suzanne, once so tenderly nurtured, it was revolting; and required all her fortitude and trust in God to enable her to submit to such a lot.

Oh! What a 'home' was that which had been provided for this unfortunate little girl, and provided too, by one who called himself a priest of God, and the servant of a merciful Saviour! Did Father Anselmo's conscience never smite him for his cruelty to that unoffending child? Did it never occur to him that his Maker would require an account of the precious life he was thus wasting, and the misery he was so wantonly inflicting? No! Father Anselmo perhaps began life with far different motives than those which actuated him now; but the heart of man is deceitful above all things; and trusting in himself alone, the Evil One gradually converted him into the malevolent being he had become; and, as time went on, he became more and more unscrupulous and cruel.

Weeks and months of wretchedness to poor little Suzanne passed away; winter was over, and spring — beautiful invigorating spring, in its turn made way for summer; and still Suzanne de l'Orme was an inmate of the brickmaker's dwelling, hoping against hope, that deliverance would come. Ill usage, and privation of every sort, insufficient food, and want of companionship, had made sad havoc on the fragile frame of the little girl, once so healthy and active. She looked worn and ill. In health or in sickness, she was compelled to labour at the hard work imposed on her — no excuse was allowed except when it suited her tormentors; but she struggled on, and did her duty.

The life she led can be imagined from the fact that some of her happiest moments were those she spent under the shadow of those great oak trees, watching the pig and the cow belonging to the establishment, and preventing their straying beyond the enclosure. On these occasions she employed herself in knitting coarse woollen stockings for Etienne and his son, thus enabling Margot to devote more time to other occupations indoors or out of doors; occupations which were less suited to Suzanne's years or strength. Sometimes, too, she employed her spare time in weeding the plot of ground which went by the name of garden, or in feeding the fowls, when she was fortunate enough to find some food fitted for them. In these innocent employments she for a while forgot her sorrows; and the mute caresses of her feathered pets, who would run to her the moment they heard her gentle voice, made up in some degree for more congenial companionship. The strip of herbage under the trees was, however, her favourite place of resort; for there, at least, she was safe from blows and bad language, and there she could think of her beloved relatives, and wonder what had become of them. On rainy days she used to creep up to her loft when not otherwise wanted, and there meditate upon her lot; and at night sweet dreams of home and friends would visit her – dreams, which, though dispelled by the morning light, still comforted the forlorn child, and enabled her to pass through the fiery trial which was imposed on her.

Old Margot still befriended her when she could do so, and often interposed between her and her tormentors, many times receiving blows which were intended for the unoffending child. Alas! She could do but little; for husband and son were prone to wreak their revenge on the poor little girl, after she had made any effort on her behalf. Had it not been for the cruel treatment she received at the hands of these men, Suzanne might in time have become reconciled to a life so full of discomfort, and to language so coarse as to be nearly unintelligible to her; so true is it that the eye becomes accustomed to sights, and the ears to sounds, from which at first they recoil in disgust; but bodily hardship and suffering were added to all else she had to endure, and this kept her from sinking to the level of those she was compelled to live with. Unhappy as her life was within doors, it was as nothing compared to what she had to endure when away from Margot's scanty protection; and she hailed, with a feeling something akin to joy, the days when the inclemency of the weather prevented the usual work in the brickfield from going on, or when business called Simon and his son to the neighbouring town.

Father Anselmo came occasionally to see if Suzanne's spirit had been conquered; but finding her still resolute and unconvinced, and having after a time other work on hand, his visits became more rare. The little girl had thus some respite from his persecutions; and she found it less difficult to bear the privations and hardships which she had to endure from the Simons, than the actual presence of the man whom she regarded as her evil genius. The priest had so much to do in trying to convert other heretics, and failing of that, in inflicting the most atrocious and unheard of punishments on them, that little by little his interest in Suzanne de l'Orme flagged; and it was only when he had disposed of others nearer home, that he indulged himself with a visit to the poor outcast, whom he had torn from her happy home, and exposed to every insult and bad treatment which the heart of man could devise. Suzanne was thus comparatively left in peace, but the dread of Father Anselmo's returning at any moment, poisoned her existence, and wore out her health and strength.

A FATHER'S PROMISE

While Suzanne de l'Orme's strength of body was gradually declining, her father was not unmindful of this promise to return for his lost child. For some time he could receive no tidings of her, and besides, his slender means forbade his even attempting to return to France. He was therefore obliged to labour incessantly and diligently, to obtain a sufficient sum to defray his expenses in travelling, and to maintain his family during his absence, which, for aught he knew, might be protracted for a considerable period. His employers had heard from some of the other refugees, the sad history of the child's abduction; and they willingly consented to his absenting himself to go in search of her – not only promising to re-employ him on his return, but contributing a sum of money to meet any unexpected calls on his purse during the journey. Early in the month of May, he received intelligence from Paul le Grand, that their vessel was again to sail with a cargo for England; and that he was welcome to take a passage to France on her return, which would be a few weeks later; that he would meet with a warm reception from his friends, and every assistance given him in prosecuting the search for his child. He accordingly made every necessary preparation, and, with much sorrow and anxiety, he left his wife and children, and embarked. The wind being fair, after a shorter voyage than he had dared to expect, he again set foot on his native soil, with feelings working in his heart, which it would be impossible to describe.

It was night when the vessel anchored, and he disembarked in a boat manned by the two le Grands, who had not trusted the secret of his coming to any other person. They well knew the danger he incurred by returning to France, for the troubles had only increased since Monsieur de l'Orme's departure; and arrests and imprisonments – aye, and even worse than these, were the lot of many an uncompromising Huguenot.

The le Grands hardly dared to breath until they were safe in the house which had once before given Monsieur de l'Orme shelter; but once within its walls, with doors barred and bolted, and shutters closed, they could, without fear, tell their friend what happiness it was to them to receive him once more under their roof.

Jeanne le Grand had remained up to receive them. She set before the weary traveller the repast he so much needed; and would have hurried him off to bed, had not Monsieur de l'Orme told her, that before doing so, he wished to have a little conversation with her brothers, as to the best mode of carrying on his researches after his unfortunate child; and, he added with a sad smile, 'when all is settled, I shall be able to sleep better. '

A slight sketch must now be given of the le Grands. Paul, the elder of the two, was about ten years younger than Monsieur de l'Orme; he did not, however, actually appear so, notwithstanding the many silver threads which sorrow had mingled with the dark hair of the latter. The naturally pale complexion of Paul was embrowned by constant exposure in the fields and on the shore, and the thoughtful gravity habitual to him, was increased by the constant dread in which the Huguenots lived, and made him look older than he really was. There was a singular likeness between him and his friend – not so much of feature, as of expression – and there was a certain air of refinement about Paul, rough as his manner of living and occupation were, perhaps accounting for a resemblance, which even those who knew them well, could not fail to observe. He was about the same height as Monsieur de l'Orme; a little stouter he might be, but not sufficiently so to be noticed.

Victor, on the contrary, was short and stout, of a merry, contented disposition, which no misfortune or danger could sadden. He was three or four years younger than Paul; and his fair complexion and bright blue eyes, formed a complete contrast to his grave elder brother. They were much attached to each other; and Victor looked up to Paul as to a being of a superior order, whilst both cherished and loved their sister Jeanne, as though she had been their mother. She indeed merited their affection, for from their earliest infancy she had brought them up with a tenderness and care, which a mother's love could scarcely have exceeded.

The conversation between the brothers and Monsieur de l'Orme was protracted to a late hour, and nothing satisfactory as to their future proceedings could be arrived at; plan after plan was discussed, and thrown aside as impracticable; when suddenly a merry laugh from Victor made the others look up inquiringly, and Paul asked what he meant by his merriment at such a time. Victor replied, 'A thought has just entered my head; why not lend Monsieur de l'Orme a suit of your clothes? You know he is very like you, and I might go with him; we have for some time past had an idea of going to buy corn to send to England, and this would be a good opportunity of doing so. I generally do all the talking, as you are not fond of expending your eloquence in that manner, and Monsieur de l'Orme need only follow your example. I'll wager any money no one will find out the difference!'

'Victor!' replied his elder brother reprovingly, 'I wonder you propose such a thing;' and turning to his guest, he said, 'Pardon my brother, Monsieur, it is only his zeal for your interest which prompted his thinking of such a scheme. '

'I have nothing to pardon, my excellent friend. On the contrary, my best thanks are due to Victor for the suggestion, and, if you have no objection, we shall act upon it as soon as may be. '

'With all my heart, but I was afraid you would think his presuming in comparing me to you; our station in life is so different to yours. '

Paul le Grand, say no more; from henceforth I look upon you and Victor as brothers; will you accept me as such?' and holding out a hand to each, the compact was sealed, never to be broken whilst life endured.

The conversation ended here, and the three friends retired to rest. The next day was devoted to making preparations for the journey; and Jeanne having been told of Victor's plan, highly approved of it. She however, remarked that Monsieur de l'Orme's complexion was scarcely so dark as Paul's, but she thought she could remedy that, when the time came for this departure. She busied herself preparing provisions for their journey, as they were to avoid stopping at any towns or villages for fear of recognition. A suit of Paul's clothes was brought out, which, although a trifle large, fitted him passing well; and Jeanne having skilfully applied some walnut juice to his face and hands, the transformation of Monsieur de l'Orme was complete. His knowledge of the 'patois' of the country proved very useful to him; for he could, if need be, converse with the people they might meet, as fluently as Paul le Grand himself.

It may seem strange that the le Grands, as Huguenots, could travel with impunity, or were left undisturbed to practice the tenets of their religion; but it must be remembered that their station in life was obscure, and their position so isolated, that few knew of their existence, or cared for their religious faith. If they did not attend one place of worship, they were supposed to be at another, and so remained unmolested, when persons of more note would have been marked for destruction. God had so over-ruled events, that it was not until sometime later that all ranks and grades of society were included in the same merciless persecution; the humble, as well as the exalted ones of the earth, were hunted from place to place, and those who escaped from the fangs of their enemies, did so after unheard of privations and anxieties. Happily for Monsieur de l'Orme, that terrible time had not yet arrived, though it was not far distant; and his friends were thus enabled to afford him assistance in the search for his daughter, which, if it had been postponed a few months later, would have been unavailable.

Everything being prepared, the travellers mounted their horses, and left the house on the following day at nightfall. It was a solemn farewell which those four people took of each other, in the uncertainty whether they should ever look upon each other's faces again. Those who remained behind knew the danger the others incurred, but not a word of dissuasion was heard; the two who were setting out on their perilous enterprise felt no fear; they had reckoned the cost, and were determined to risk everything in the attainment of their object; and trusting in the protection of an over-ruling providence, they parted from their friends, and set forth on their journey.

The road which the two friends took was the same as that which had been pursued by Pierre de l'Orme and his family when they fled from their home; but now being unencumbered with women and children, they travelled with greater speed, always careful however to avoid observation. They stopped occasionally in some unfrequented spot to rest their horses, and to partake of the food provided for them by the careful Jeanne; and owing to the precautions they took, at length arrived in the neighbourhood of Saumur without accident of any kind,

and immediately proceeded to the house of an uncle of the le
Grands, who owned a windmill on the height overlooking the
town, and whose dwelling was built close to it.

Jacques Michel had long expected their arrival, for it was
through him that intelligence had been received from time
to time with regard to poor little Suzanne. He was a worthy
man, always ready to do a good turn to those who needed it.
He had hitherto been left unmolested, although he professed
the Reformed faith, as well as the other members of his family.
When any one remarked that it was strange he was so long
left in peace, he would say, 'that the Papists wanted their corn
ground at his mill, and he supposed that was the reason they
did not meddle with him. 'This might be the truth; but another,
and more forcible reason was, that Jacques Michel was a man
of stalwart proportions and gigantic strength, and it might have
fared hard with any one who would have attempted to molest
him; moreover, he kept very quiet, and intruded his opinions on
nobody. He was a married man, without children, and his wife,
a good-humoured brisk little woman, kept his house and himself
in the most perfect order.

It was dusk when the travellers presented themselves at
Michel's door; for, afraid of recognition, they had waited until
the shades of evening had deepened, and still further prevented
curious passers-by from observing them.

Having knocked at the door, Jacques himself opened it.
Although he knew it was the intention of Monsieur de l'Orme
to come and search for his lost child, yet so complete was his
disguise, that Jacques thought the poor father had given up the
attempt in despair, and that it was his two nephews who stood
before him. He was soon undeceived; and the two friends entered
Jacques Michel's house with a feeling of deep thankfulness for
the protection given to them so far. Having partaken of the good
miller's hospitality, he proceeded to tell them everything which
had been ascertained by himself and others respecting little
Suzanne. It was but little after all, still that little was a help.

Soon after the departure of the de l'Ormes for England, Jacques Michel was told that a little girl had been seen in company with two priests walking in the direction of St. Anne's. The person who saw them was too far off to recognise the child; and indeed thought little of the circumstances at the time, as it was not unusual for children belonging to their parishioners, to be noticed by those who attended to their religious instruction.

The person who had observed this, was at the time on his way to a distant town, whither he was going on business. On his return, hearing of poor little Suzanne's disappearance, he told Michel what he had seen. Michel at once went to apprise Monsieur Morin of this; and slight as the clue was, the good pastor resolved to follow it up, and discover, if possible, where the poor little girl had been hidden. He accordingly made many inquiries, but he was obliged to be very cautious, for fear of being suspected himself, and for a long time he was unsuccessful.

About this period he received a message from some of his Huguenot brethren, to the effect, that his presence was much needed at a village some leagues further; and if he could come with safety, praying him to do so. Monsieur Morin was always ready to help the distressed, and at this moment had more leisure on his hands than he liked; for the services of his Church having been prohibited, he could no longer assemble his beloved flock, as had been his want. The only thing which could be accomplished now, was meeting a few at a time in the cottages of the Reformers, there to join in prayer and supplication to God, entreating Him to send them peace and freedom from persecution. These meetings, however, could only be held by stealth, and at long intervals, for fear of detection.

The good pastor having therefore paid a farewell visit to Jacques Michel, and enjoined him to keep a vigilant watch over the neighbouring country, and to take note of every passing rumour respecting Mademoiselle de l'Orme, began his journey, choosing bye-paths, and unfrequented lanes in preference to the high road, as affording greater concealment.

It was about mid-day when he left the mill; and the weather being warm, he walked slowly, musing as he went along on the troubles which had fallen on himself and his co-religionists. His mind took a retrospective view of the years which were passed and he pondered with intense sorrow on the havoc which the bigotry and wickedness of man had made in the prosperity of most of the districts where the Reformed faith had not only been tolerated, but upheld and encouraged.

More particularly, he thought of his native town. Saumur had for many years been a stronghold of the Huguenots, thousands of whom had come to settle there from all parts of France, and even from Switzerland. In those days the prosperity of the town was extraordinary; artisans of all classes flocked there, and, under the Edict of Nantes, carried on extensive manufactures of various kinds, which contributed to the wealth and importance of the place. The cancelling of that edict was ruinous in its effects, and Monsieur Morin sighed often as he thought of the insignificance to which his beloved Saumur was reduced. Few, comparatively few, of the Huguenots had remained within its walls, all who could do so seeking safety in flight.

As he went along he was obliged for a short space to diverge into the high road; but he had hardly done so, when he perceived in the distance two persons coming towards him. He fancied they looked like ecclesiastics, and, wishing to avoid observation, he took advantage of a gap in the hedge which bordered the road, to step aside into a field, and there conceal himself whilst they passed. The priests (for such they proved to be) fortunately did not observe him. In the first place, they were too much engrossed by their conversation, and, secondly, they were at too great a distance to recognise anybody. Besides, he disappeared so soon that there was scarcely time for them even to notice him. Monsieur Morin, from having been hunted so often, had learned quickness of action, and quietness of motion. Notwithstanding his great age, he was a very active man, and this stood him in good stead now.

He sat down on the trunk of a fallen tree, scarcely daring to breathe until the danger was passed. At last the footsteps of the persons he observed became audible, and the sound of their voices fell on Monsieur Morin's ear. Thinking themselves alone, not a creature being in sight, they were not careful to modulate their tones; but still the good pastor could not make out the purport of their conversation. He did not desire to do so, thinking it could not possibly interest him, and was only impatient that they should go on their way as soon as might be, as he was anxious to resume his journey. He was a courageous old man: but a feeling of terror came involuntarily over him, when, just as they must have reached the other side of the hedge, in line with his place of concealment, he heard the footsteps of the two men stop.

Monsieur Morin expected every moment to see them standing before him, fancying they must have observed his disappearance from the road; and if so, his doom was sealed. Not so, however; they were totally unconscious that any human being near, and had only stopped that the elder of the two priests might give more force to an observation he was making to his companion.

Monsieur Morin's attention was riveted by hearing the following words – 'I tell you, brother Antoine, I am resolved to conquer her spirit! I have never been thwarted yet, when I have set my mind on the attainment of any object; and the obstinacy of this little heretic has roused me to such a pitch, that she *shall* obey me before she is much older, or my name is not Anselmo.'

Monsieur Morin had heard this speech with breathless attention; and before the speaker had finished his sentence, he had recognised his voice as one, the tones of which were familiar to him. He could not, in the trepidation of the moment, fix upon the person to whom that voice belonged; but the incautious manner in which Father Anselmo proclaimed his name and intentions enlightened at once the good pastor; and made him aware, that he was standing within a few feet of one of the most cruel and unscrupulous enemies of the Reformed religion. It was therefore in fear and trembling that he listened for what might follow, hoping it would lead to some clue for discovering the lost child. After a moment's pause, he heard the other person reply, 'Poor little girl! Her fate seems hard; one cannot but admire her constancy, however much one may deplore her errors. She is very young to have gone through so much sorrow and suffering!'

'Upon my word, brother Antoine, your sympathy seems to me strangely misplaced. I fancy if you often go to see her, you will yourself become a convert to her absurd faith!'

'You misunderstand me, Father,' replied, the young priest, who accompanied his superior, 'I could not possibly become a convert to a faith in which I do not believe; at any rate, it would require more profound arguments than those which a child of twelve years of age could bring forward. From my earliest childhood, I have been taught to look up to this only true Church. But surely the sight of such genuine piety as that which we have witnessed this day, ought to inspire admiration even from those who believe the child to be a heretic. 'This was a bold speech; but brother Antoine, with all his gentleness and kindliness of disposition, was a brave man, and could stand up in defence of the oppressed when it was needed; and in this instance he forgot his own safety, in pity for the poor persecuted little girl. He was recalled to a sense of his danger, by the sneering exclamation of his elder priest. 'You are eloquent, my son; but Mademoiselle' – here the speaker's voice became indistinct, himself and his companion having resumed their journey.

Monsieur Morin was stupefied by what he had just heard; but not a doubt remained on his mind as to whom the two priests alluded. Where, however, was the hapless child concealed? Her jailer (for Father Anselmo acted that part to her) had moved an instant too soon; he might, had he remained longer, have revealed her place of abode; there was a possibility that he would have done so, but the opportunity was lost, and Monsieur Morin was as much in the dark as before.

This was, however, another clue, and perhaps he might, by this slender thread find his way into the maze where Suzanne was imprisoned.

The good old man thanked God fervently for having inspired him with the thought of going into that field; and cautiously reconnoitring the road to see that it was clear of obstacles, he again set out with hope strong in his heart, and a full determination to find the child, if it was in his power to do so.

In a short time Monsieur Morin came to a place where four roads met. The one to the left led directly to the town whither he was bound; he hesitated a moment, but reflecting that the business which called him away was urgent, he determined to do his duty first, and perhaps on his road thither he might hear something which might lead to Suzanne's discovery. Had he taken the turning to the right, he would have seen a quarter of a mile farther a child sobbing out her grief and terror, at the threats and maledictions which had been showered on her, some two hours before, by the very Father Anselmo he had heard speaking from his hiding place in the field. Yes! Little Suzanne was very near him, although he knew it not; and he went his way unsuspectingly, little dreaming of what he had missed, and how very long it would be ere he could revisit the part of the country he was now leaving.

When he arrived at his destination, he was sent on a mission to a far off part of France; but before leaving, he wrote a few words to Jacques Michel, telling him what he had overheard, and he begged one of his friends to transmit the letter to him as soon as he could do so with safety.

That letter never reached its destination, the poor Huguenot having been forced to fly at a moment's warning; and fearing it might fall into the hands of enemies – he destroyed it. Thus Jacques Michel remained in ignorance of what would have been valuable information, and consequently Monsieur de l'Orme and his companion had to begin their search with very small means of attaining their object.

SEARCH AFRESH

After a night's rest at the mill, these two enterprising and devoted men began their labour of love; and at early dawn they were up and doing. For many days they wandered cautiously up and down the country; but somehow, they always went in the neighbourhood of St. Anne's, supposing the child would be more likely found there than in any other place. They were mistaken. Father Anselmo had taken his victim in a directly opposite direction to the convent; and thus, for want of proper information much time was lost.

A week or two was spent in this way. Monsieur de l'Orme and his companion were beginning to lose hope, - so fruitless had their exertions been hitherto, - but the former was determined to devote even months, if necessary, to the purpose which had brought him back to France. He tried, however, to persuade Victor to return home, as he knew his brother would want him;

but Victor was inexorable, and pleaded so earnestly to be allowed to remain, that his friend yielded to his wishes, and was only too glad to keep him.

They went once to visit Pierre de l'Orme's former home. They chose the night for doing so; and the light of the moon, as it fitfully gleamed on the desolate abode, made it look so weird and ghost-like, as it stood in its loneliness and decay, that its once happy owner felt quite dejected. No one had lived in it since he and his family had left; and the idlers of the neighbouring village had amused themselves in casting stones and mud into the windows, by way of showing the detestation of the religion of its former occupants. The latticed panes were broken, and the plaster on the walls falling off; the roof had given way in many parts, and looked in a very ruinous condition; whilst the pretty creeping plants which had adorned the porch, and which it had been Madeleine de l'Orme's pride to train and coax into every graceful position, were torn down and trampled under foot. In the garden, tall weeds and nettles grew in rank disorder, and took the place of the flowers which had grown there; and the once neatly kept gravel path was now nearly impassable from the heaps of stones and rubbish which had been hurled there by the senseless fanatics of the place. Poor Monsieur de l'Orme's feelings were harrowed beyond description, at seeing the desecration of his home; but he would not have gone back to England without visiting, once more, the place hallowed by so many tender recollections. It had been the cradle of his infancy – the paradise of his childhood and early youth, when he was ignorant of the troubles which lowered on the horizon – and the cherished and beloved home of his riper years, when wife and children added fresh happiness to that which he had already possessed. We have seen how little by little this happiness was clouded; and how rudely he had been torn from the place of his birth and affections; it was, therefore, no wonder that the grave and usually self-possessed Huguenot, for once, gave way to the emotion which overpowered him. The struggle was short and sharp, and he soon recovered himself; but this visit to the home of his ancestors so saddened Pierre de l'Orme, that his friends persuaded him to return there no more, and he yielded to their persuasions. Well was it for him that he allowed himself to be over-ruled; for along that road passed Father Anselmo at all hours and seasons, and his penetration would soon have seen through the disguise assumed by Monsieur de l'Orme.

One evening Jacques Michel suggested their going on with their search in a totally different direction; for, he argued, 'if the child cannot be found in the part of the country you have already so minutely explored, she may perhaps be across the river. She is not at the convent itself – of that I am pretty well assured; my wife knows the portress, and sometimes has occasion to go to the convent gate, to receive payment for the corn which I grind for the nuns; and as the good woman is a sort of gossip in her way, Jacqueline sometimes gets a bit of news from her. At the time of Mademoiselle de l'Orme's unaccountable disappearance, she let out, thanks to her talkative propensities, that sometimes children had been taken there; once in particular, a young girl had been brought, but she had not remained there long – whilst there, however, she had been kindly treated, but was soon taken away, and carried she knew not whither – then, seeing an inquisitive look on my wife's face, she stopped short, fancying she had said quite enough; then added, - "but that happened several years ago. "To every other question which was put to her she returned an evasive answer; and finding nothing more could be elicited from her, my wife came away not much wiser than when she went. My opinion, however, is, that you should *try* that direction,' and he indicated the place he meant. 'Something tells me that Mademoiselle might be found there; it is a strange idea, and there may be nothing in it, but there will be no harm to follow it up, and see what will come of it. '

It was accordingly decided that the next morning they should begin their search afresh; and after a hasty breakfast they resumed their wanderings. This time they pursued the road taken by Monsieur Morin, the only difference being – that they kept to the highway, which shortened the distance considerably.

When they came to the four roads where the good pastor had stopped to consider, they did the same; but instead of taking the turning to the left, they went straight on, and about a mile farther they came to a village. Here they stayed to rest, and having taken some refreshment, they sat on a bench outside the little hostelry, to decide on what was next to be done. Overcome with fatigue, and the heat of the weather, Victor fell asleep; not so Monsieur de l'Orme, his mind was too much preoccupied to allow him to follow his friend's example, and after waiting sometime lost in thought, he at last roused himself, but, unwilling to disturb the sleeper, he left him without a word, and sauntered along a road which was almost immediately opposite the place where they were sitting.

He pursued this road for about half a mile, and then came to a brick-field. Had he turned to the right, he would have come back to the place where Victor and himself had stopped to consider which way they would proceed; but instead he turned to the left, and at the end of the brick-field, he entered a narrow lane, the one we have before described. He wandered on, his mind full of sad thoughts; all at once his attention was arrested by a childish voice; the sound seemed familiar to him, and he listened attentively.

His feelings may be better imagined than described, when he heard, in accents of intense anguish, the words, 'My God! Oh my God! Have pity upon me; leave me not to die in this place! Send my dear father to fetch me!'

Pierre de l'Orme's heart stood still; then with an unuttered thanksgiving to Him who had guided his steps thither, he breathed once more. Cautiously climbing the hedge, he looked between the bushes; and on her knees, beneath the shade of the great oak trees, he saw a little girl: could she be his child, his beloved Suzanne? At first he could not believe it; but the tones of that voice could not be mistaken, as the poor forlorn one still poured forth her prayer for deliverance to her Father in Heaven. Poor child! She was indeed changed! Her frame was thin and emaciated, and her face wan and colourless; her eyes, once so soft and beautiful, were dimmed with weeping, and encircled by shadows so deep as to make them appear yet more sunken than they actually were. No wonder, then, that Monsieur de l'Orme had trouble to recognise his fair child in the wreck which appeared before him; but he could not doubt; - that voice could belong to no one but his Suzanne, and her prayer alone would have satisfied him that his search was ended.

As soon as she ceased speaking, he ventured on pronouncing her name in a low tone; she gave a startled look, but not quite in the direction where he was standing. Again Monsieur de l'Orme repeated the word 'Suzanne!' And raising himself a little higher than he had done before, the child saw him. For one moment it seemed almost more than she could bear – her eyes dilated – her senses appeared to be forsaking her, and with a stifled cry she fell back. To spring over the hedge was the work of an instant, and Pierre de l'Orme, raising his daughter in his arms, took a small flask of wine which he fortunately had in his pocket, and poured some of its contents down her throat. This revived her, and then father and child indulged in caresses and endearments, such as perhaps the grave Huguenot might at another moment have deemed unseemly.

For a short time they both forgot the danger to which they were exposed; but at length Monsieur de l'Orme remembered that extreme caution was still necessary, or that the treasure he had but now recovered might be again snatched from his grasp never to be restored. He accordingly returned to his hiding-place in the lane, and there held a consultation with his daughter as to the best means of removing her from her bondage.

In a few words she told him of the hard work she had to do – of the heavy loads she had to carry with Mathurin Simon, and of the unbearably miserable life it would have been, but for the protection and help which God had given her throughout, and how He had inspired old Margot with feelings of kindness for her which made her existence less burdensome than it would otherwise have been. Sad, unspeakably sad, had been the existence of this patient child. Often and often had she nearly sunk under the ill-treatment she received at the hands of her taskmasters; once in particular, when her tottering limbs refused to sustain her, and she fell beneath the load which she in vain tried to carry, she was compelled to rise by the inhuman monster who had shared the burden with her, and although almost fainting from exhaustion, she was made to replace the bricks on the barrow from which they had fallen. Some had been damaged by the fall, and this so enraged Mathurin, that, seizing a stick, he struck the poor defenceless girl savagely. His mother, hearing the noise he made, came out and interposed between him and the prostrate child; she clung to his uplifted arm and saved her from blows, the weight of which would assuredly have killed her; and when at last his fury was quelled, she carried the almost senseless victim into the house, and tended her to he best of her ability.

Many such scenes and outrages, alas! Suzanne de l'Orme was subjected to, and any one with common feeling must have seen, that if her sojourn in the place were long protracted, she would sink under the load of oppression which she had to bear.

All this Suzanne told in her own simple way; never boasting of her patience and piety; and as her father listened to her recital, he thanked God in his inmost heart for having given him such a heroic, pure-minded child. He was prouder of her in her rags, and with her toil-stained face and hands, than if she had been arrayed in the costliest raiment.

Few indeed would have recognised Suzanne de l'Orme in her present garb – a striped woollen petticoat, such as was worn by the poorest of the village children, torn and dirty; a blue cotton bodice, which, notwithstanding her utmost care, was rent in many places, and surmounted by a red and yellow kerchief crossed under her arms – an apron of the coarsest cloth, and her once luxuriant and shining hair, now matted and tangled, was partly concealed by a soiled cap, without border, fitting close to her head. Her poor stockingless feet, full of bruises and sores, were thrust into a pair of wooden shoes, or 'sabots' Margot had given her during the winter, with a pair of coarse woollen stockings, which had once belonged to her dead child; and great was the boon to poor Suzanne, for old and ragged as they were, they still kept up a degree of warmth in her benumbed feet – now, she had no need of them, and they were carefully put aside in case she should want them again.

As Pierre de l'Orme gazed on the sad picture before him, and listened to the artless tale of his daughter's sufferings, his indignation knew no bounds. He clenched his hands together, as if to still the tempest that raged within him, and for some moments forgot the Christian charity with which he usually regarded the most faulty of mankind; he was indeed a true Christian, but he was a father also; every fibre in his frame tingled with anger, as he looked on the emaciated form of his once blooming child; and had Father Anselmo appeared at that moment, the sacred character of his office would not have shielded him from the wrath of the indignant parent, and Pierre de l'Orme might have done *that*, which a whole after-life of repentance could not have atoned for. Well was it for him then, that the cruel and crafty priest was far away; or the words, 'Vengeance is Mine, I will repay, saith the Lord,' might have been lost sight of.

A few moments of reflection calmed the poor father's emotion, and he could listen to Suzanne once more, and make plans for her deliverance. All around them was very still, nothing was heard but the twittering of the birds in the branches overhead, or the occasional lowing of the cows in some neighbouring pasture; the sky was serenely blue, and the sun shone brightly; nothing seemed to mar the fair scene which stretched far and wide, and few could have guessed the load of sorrow which oppressed many a homestead in that beautiful country.

God had created it in its unrivalled loveliness, but the ruthless hand of man had spread desolation over multitudes of happy homes; and families without number were scattered over the face of the earth, in countries perhaps as fair, but never to them like their own dear fatherland. To many, probably, the affliction was necessary – to all, it was salutary; for it taught them the instability of all things temporal, and made them look beyond this world to that blessed land, where there are no partings or sorrows, and where tears are wiped away.

Thoughts such as these passed quickly through the mind of Monsieur de l'Orme, as he beheld his hapless child. He had bitter experience of what those who serve God truly are to expect in times of persecution at the hands of His enemies; and her father was learning a lesson of patience and submission to the will of the Almighty, by the example of that poor little suffering girl. He breathed a prayer for guidance in the difficult task before him – the rescue of Suzanne from bondage; and he proceeded to discuss with her the means most likely to succeed in conveying her away from the place.

He was naturally anxious to know how it happened she was left so long at liberty. Suzanne told him that Etienne Simon and his son had left early that morning for a town where a fair was being held, and were not expected home until nightfall.

'But, my child, are you sure no one can observe us?'

'Oh, no, dear father, Margot is very busy within the house, and there is no one else about the place but old Marcel, who has been left to mind the kiln. He is quite deaf, and nearly blind – there he is now at the other end of the field, and he cannot see us; but, father, are you not going to take me with you?'

'Would that I could, my Suzanne; but it would be madness to do so now. Somebody would be sure to see us; you would be torn from me, and all my endeavours to deliver you would be fruitless; for you know that once in the hands of our enemies, I should be cast into prison, and perhaps death would be the consequence: most probably it would, for the cruel man who has so long oppressed you, would leave no stone unturned to compass my destruction.'

Suzanne shuddered, for she well knew the remorseless character of Father Anselmo; but the poor child could not conceal the dismay she felt at being once more left alone.

Her father seeing her distress, begged her to remember her sorrowing mother; 'and,' he added, 'you have always been an obedient and loving child; you will believe, therefore, that what I purpose doing is for the best. Will you not, my Suzanne?'

With quivering lips and gasping utterance she articulated, 'Yes, dear father, I am ready to wait until you think fit to come for me.'

'My brave little girl! Trust me for coming as soon as possible; God will help me to find the means of doing so – and now, tell me where you sleep?'

'In the loft over that stable, Father,' she replied, pointing to the place where she had spent so many solitary nights; 'but I shall not be able to come to you, for there is no way of going up or down but by a ladder, which is taken away as soon as I am in the loft, and carried into the house, for fear I should try to escape.'

'Never mind, Suzanne, I shall find ways and means of getting at you; but tell me, can you keep awake till midnight? I have a friend at the village yonder, and he will help me to carry you off; but if you should go to sleep I would have to call, perhaps in a loud voice, and other might hear as well as yourself.'

'Dear Father, do you think I could sleep with the prospect of so soon seeing you again, and with the hope of leaving a place where I have been so miserable? There is no fear of my falling asleep.'

'Tell me, Suzanne, are there no dogs on the premises?'

'Oh! Yes – we have two – I had forgotten them; but I have seen nothing of them to-day, so I suppose they followed Maître Etienne and Mathurin, when they left this morning. What is to be done: for they bark furiously if any one approaches the house?'

'I must provide for that,' said Monsieur de l'Orme; 'no dogs shall stand between me and my child. You are sure you will keep awake, Suzanne?'

'Yes, dear Father, do not be uneasy.'

'Then I must say farewell now – it is not for long, and I have many arrangements to make with Victor le Grand – time is passing and I have much to do. Adieu, then, my beloved child, for a few short hours.'

'Is Victor le Grand with you, father? Oh, I am so glad!'

'Yes, my daughter! He has kindly assisted me in my long search for you.'

Having looked round cautiously, Pierre de l'Orme once more sprang over the hedge; and, having imprinted a fervent kiss on his child's cheek, he, after commending her to the protection of the Almighty, went back to the village where he had left his companion.

RESCUE PLAN

Monsieur de l'Orme no longer loitered on the way; his feet seemed winged, so swiftly did he retrace his steps; and although it has taken a long time to describe the foregoing occurrences, it was comparatively short in reality. Victor was just awaking when his friend re-appeared; indeed he was not fully awake, for he actually started when Pierre de l'Orme, laying his hand on his shoulder, exclaimed, 'What, sleeping still!'

There was something so unusual, so joyous in the sound of Pierre de l'Orme's voice that Victor's attention was at once arrested. 'What is the matter? What has occurred? Have you found her?'

'I have!' Was the answer; and Monsieur de l'Orme proceeded to relate what had happened since he left the auberge. There was no time to be lost, so it was resolved that Victor should at once return to Michel's house, apprise them of their success, and come back immediately with the two horses.

To save time Monsieur de l'Orme walked part of the way with him, tired though he was; and as they walked they perfected their plans about carrying off Suzanne. The anxious father could not tear himself away from the neighbourhood of his child; and it was determined that he should remain concealed in the vicinity of the brick-maker's house, so that should danger arise, he might be at hand to rescue his daughter. Both Victor and himself were armed with pistols concealed beneath vests, but hitherto they had not wanted them. Now, however, they examined them carefully, for the time might be at hand when force would probably be needed; and although, if possible, it was their intention to avoid bloodshed, still they might be attacked; and they determined to defend themselves to the utmost of their ability, and sell their lives as dearly as they could.

Having satisfied themselves that their weapons were in order, they replaced them in their belts; and drawing their long vests over them, they looked what they were in reality, notwithstanding their warlike accoutrements – men of peace.

The next thing to be decided upon was the place of rendezvous. Monsieur de l'Orme thought it wiser to proceed alone, and on foot, to the rescue of his daughter; the noise of horses' feet at that hour being likely to attract attention, and lead to inquiry.

It was therefore resolved that Victor having brought the horses through the most unfrequented ways leading to the place, should halt in a forest about half a mile to the left of the village, and there wait until his companion should join him with his rescued child. They turned aside into this forest, and fixed on the place of meeting; and everything being arranged satisfactorily, the friends parted, full of hope for the success of their undertaking.

Monsieur de l'Orme now retraced his steps towards the village; but being afraid of again visiting the little auberge for fear of attracting notice, he diverged into a lane leading in the direction of Simon's; house; and there, hiding amongst the trees and bushes, awaited the hour fixed for his enterprise.

As the time passed on he began to feel hungry, but he dared not go anywhere to procure food, as it might have excited suspicion and led to discovery. He felt in his pocket, and there discovered a piece of bread, and that, with a portion of the wine remaining in his flask, sustained him for some hours.

Night closed in. He took his station in the lane from whence he had discovered his daughter, and quietly ensconcing himself among the thick brushwood on the hedge, he passed the intervening time until the period of Suzanne's deliverance arrived.

How beautiful was the night! The stars came out one by one, and the young moon shed her mild peaceful rays over the sleeping landscape. Little by little, all worldly sounds died away; the lights in the far off cottages were extinguished, and naught was heard but the chirp of the cricket, and the indescribable sound of the insect world, roaming about in search of its prey. As Pierre de l'Orme gazed on the myriads of stars which irradiated the firmament, he lifted his heart in adoration to the Great Being whose work they are, and from its inmost depths arose the words of the Psalmist, 'Lord, how wonderful are Thy works: in wisdom hast Thou made them all. '

As he meditated on the inscrutable ways of the Almighty, the assurance was given, that his child would be restored to him; and a peace so perfect stole over him, that from that moment he felt no doubt as to the ultimate result of his bold undertaking. Hour after hour he watched from his hiding-place, and he even saw Suzanne leave the house accompanied by Margot. Before entering the stable, the old woman laid her hand on the child's head, as if caressingly; and he even fancied she stooped down to kiss her. It was no fancy, for Margot actually did so, for the first time since Suzanne had so strangely become an inmate of her dwelling. Had she a presentiment that she would see her no more? Perhaps so; but certain it is, that before bidding her 'good night,' she looked at the child long and fixedly; and seeing something in her face which she had never noticed before – a sort of shadowy beauty lighting up her emaciated features, she said within herself, 'Poor child! You will not be long with us.' Her thoughts were prophetic; but not in the sense she meant them. She imagined that the look of quiet happiness which pervaded the whole manner of the little girl was the forerunner of an early death – she did not know what had occurred that afternoon to make the poor outcast's heart rejoice with such exceeding joy that her whole frame seemed pervaded with its exhilarating influence; and so, with a kindly, 'bon soir,' they parted – Suzanne sorry that she could not confide her near departure to the only friend she had known during her sojourn in that miserable place; but feeling the impossibility of imparting, even to her.

As Pierre de l'Orme witnessed the caressing gesture of the poor woman, he invoked a blessing on her, for her kindness to his child. Surely it was heard, and she felt the effects of that blessing in after life.

THUS FAR AND NO FARTHER

Whilst the anxious father was waiting and watching, let us see how the last few days had been spent by Suzanne de l'Orme. The child was growing gradually weaker, and less able to bear the burden which was laid upon her; but she did not complain. She meekly obeyed when she was ordered about by her cruel task-masters, and did their bidding to the utmost of her ability.

The day before her father's arrival she had an unexpected visit from Father Anselmo, who had again tried his powers of persuasion on her; finding them unavailing, his patience quite deserted him, and he, as usual, had recourse to threats and denunciations. This being equally ineffectual, he became so exasperated, that he actually raised his hand to strike the poor little girl. Something, however, in her eye stayed his uplifted hand – she was spared the blow – and he, the sin of having inflicted it. He looked menacingly at her, and said, 'You will repent this obstinacy;' after a moment's reflection, he added, 'I shall find another home for you, where perhaps your proud spirit may learn to bend, and where you will have no one to indulge your fancies in anyway. '

The cunning man had discovered old Margot's kindness to the child, slight though it was, and he was determined to deprive her even of that comfort. In the absorbing wish to compass what his corrupt heart had imagined, he forgot that his actions were subject to a Higher Power; and the words, 'l'homme propose, mais Dieu dispose,' were as a dead letter to him; and in the wicked pride of his heart he made plans which were never to be realized. He made sure of his little prisoner, and went his way to mature the means of placing her with others, still more subservient to his will than the Simons were; but God's decree had gone forth, 'Thus far shalt thou go, and no farther;' and whilst he was pondering on her future lot, his intended victim was far away from his power, never more to see him again.

The foregoing incident occurred the day before Suzanne's father discovered the place of her concealment. Surely God guided him and his companion, and influenced them in making the search for her on that day, and in that direction.

Let us now return to Monsieur de l'Orme. He continued his watch untiringly; no human being was now abroad with the exception of old Margot, who came ever and anon, to look out for her husband and son; and he at last could not have seen her, but for the light which shone behind her, as she opened the house-door. At length she seemed satisfied that there was no hope of their return, for she shut herself in, and having extinguished her lamp, all was left in darkness and silence. As Pierre listened to the hours striking one after another from the village clock, he wondered what could keep the men from returning home, but he felt thankful that such was the case, as it was one obstacle less in his way.

Midnight at length sounded on his ear; and, with an expression of deep gratitude that the moment of his daughter's deliverance had at last arrived, he prepared for action. Cautiously he emerged from his hiding-place, and walking softly across that portion of the field in the direction of the stable, he entered it. The door was only latched; removing the ladder being considered a sufficient precaution against her escape. Monsieur de l'Orme groping his way in, called Suzanne in a low tone. She answered immediately, and the sound of her voice at once indicated in what part of the building she was.

'I am awake, dear father; there is a hole just here, through which I creep up to my bed; but how am I to get down?'

'Jump into my arms, Suzanne; you are not afraid, are you?'

'Oh, no; but can you see me?'

'Not very distinctly, my child; but my eyes are getting accustomed to the gloom of the place, and I feel sure I shall be able to catch you as you fall; now, Suzanne, jump!'

The child did so, and was received in the loving embrace of her father, who pressed her to his heart with a thanksgiving too deep even for words. At once they left the stable, and having crossed the brickfield, they entered the lane. Pierre de l'Orme carried his recovered treasure all the way; and she, nestling in his arms in perfect security, told him in soft whispers of her happiness, and talked unceasingly of her mother and the little ones, until he, from sheer fatigue, was obliged to sit down by the road side to rest. Although Suzanne was but a shadow of her former self, and would have been a light weight for a strong man, still it must be remembered that her father had passed many hours without food, that he had undergone a great deal of fatigue during the day, and that he was still suffering from the cramped position he had been in during his long vigil; his daughter's slight weight therefore nearly proved too much for his strength. He once more had recourse to his flask of wine; and having made Suzanne take some also, after a few moments rest, they proceeded on their journey. Suzanne could not walk far, for she was barefooted, having been obliged to leave her 'sabots' behind for fear of waking Margot by their noise, and her father was compelled to take her up in his arms again and again.

At last they reached the entrance of the forest. Here Monsieur de l'Orme became so exhausted, he felt as if he could not walk one step farther, and there they stopped afresh to rest.

'Suzanne, my strength is well-nigh spent, and how we are to reach the place where Victor is I know not. Tell me, my daughter, would you be afraid of remaining here by yourself for some time, whilst I go in search of our friend? We could then bring the horses, and take you up here; and not having you to carry, I could go much faster. Do you think you would be very much frightened, Suzanne?'

'No, Father, not very much. I have been accustomed to solitude lately; besides, what could harm me? God will watch over me, and I shall not feel lonely. Do not fear, dearest Father.'

'My child, I do not like to leave you thus; but I feel it is our only chance of reaching Victor. When I came with him to choose our place of meeting, I noticed an old elm tree, the trunk of which was completely hollow. I looked at it curiously, little thinking whose resting-place it would be; it strikes me now it would be a safe refuge for my poor tired little girl. Will you come a few paces farther. If I mistake not, it is quite near this. '

Suzanne expressed her willingness to do as her father wished, and in a few moments the tree was found. Monsieur de l'Orme having taken off his coat, wrapped it round her, notwithstanding her earnest entreaties to the contrary. Placing her in the hollow, which was sufficiently large for her to stand in comfortably, and having taken leave of her, he proceeded to look for his companion. He walked as fast as he could, for he did not like the thought of that poor little girl being left alone in the forest at such an hour; and truth to tell, it would have been enough to terrify most children. Suzanne, was not, however, an ordinary child, and the trials she had gone through had ripened her understanding. Her thoughts and feelings, therefore, were more those of a woman of twenty than of a girl of thirteen.

She nevertheless felt a sort of awe stealing over her as she heard her father's receding footsteps; and it required all her faith in God's goodness to still the beating of her heart. She passed the time in thinking of her mother, and the brothers and sisters she hoped so soon to see; and after the lapse of half-an-hour, she had the satisfaction of hearing the sound of horses' hoofs in the direction which her father had taken when he left her. Not a word did she utter, for fear others besides friends might have been riding through the forest; and only when Monsieur de l'Orme pronounced her name in a low tone, did she answer, 'I am here, my Father!'

'Thank God, you are safe! Oh, Suzanne! I have been very anxious about you. '

Having dismounted, he came to her and lifted her out of the tree, and then she saw by the indistinct light that her father had two companions instead of one. A few words explained the circumstance. Good Jacques Michel had insisted on accompanying his nephew, foreseeing that difficulties and dangers might arise; that Monsieur de l'Orme being encumbered with his child, would not have the power of using his weapons if attacked, and that it would be well to have somebody besides Victor to act for him during any emergency.

Accordingly, the sturdy miller mounted his horse; and having provided himself with a well-stored wallet, in which provisions of various sorts were placed by his kind-hearted wife, he left with the assurance that he would return as soon as he possibly could.

At once honest Jacques came forward, and offered Suzanne some refreshment; and feeling strengthened by the nourishing food which he had brought, she declared herself ready to proceed on their journey. She was placed on a 'pillion' behind her father, and secured from falling by a leather strap passed under her arms and buckled round his waist.

The miller, being acquainted with all the intricacies of the forest, led the way; Monsieur de l'Orme followed, and Victor brought up the rear. It was a large forest, and many days were occupied in traversing it, burdened as they were with that poor feeble girl. It was, however, much the safer way of getting to their journey's end, and thus they chose it in preference to the more direct road.

Little now remains of the forest. Modern improvements and innovations have swept away the greater part of the beautiful trees which then grew so profusely and luxuriantly. Villages and farms have spring up in the quiet glades, and the shriek of the railway engine, as the train rushes past, is heard, where, in days gone by, all was solitary and undisturbed. Enough, however, remains to show what once existed. Groups of magnificent trees may still be seen in many places, but Suzanne's ancient elm has entirely vanished from the face of the earth; and if she and her companions could re-visit the site of that grand old forest, they would have trouble to recognise any place which they then traversed.

After riding for a couple of hours the day began to dawn; and as the sun rose in all his splendour, the travellers gazed in admiration at the wonderful beauty of the scene. Long lines of tremulous light darted through the branches overhead, and illuminated, as if by magic, the shadowy depths of the forest. Flowers of every hue opened their petals to greet the returning day; and the grass, laden with the dews of night, exhaled the most fragrant odours, whilst from every bush and brake, thousands of birds warbled forth in sweet concert, a hymn of joy and gladness in praise of their great Creator.

It was a scene calculated to raise the thoughts from earth to heaven; and with hearts filled with reverence and love, our travellers offered up fervent prayers and thanksgivings to their heavenly Father for the protection so far vouchsafed to them.

Having arrived at a quiet sequestered spot, they dismounted in order that Suzanne might have some rest, and also thinking it more prudent to remain concealed during the hours of daylight.

It was arranged that one of them should keep guard whilst the others slept; and a couch was at once improvised in a shady place for the little girl. Jacques Michel insisted on keeping the first watch; and after attending to the horses, he came and sat down by his companions. Suzanne was at first very restless, which the good man perceiving, he begged her to try to sleep. She sighed, and her eyes filled with tears. 'Ah, Monsieur Michel,' she said, 'I cannot help thinking of old Margot; she will soon find out that I have left the place, and she will be very uneasy. You cannot think how kind she has been to me, and I know she will miss me. Poor old woman! If I could only have told her I was going to leave, I should have felt happier.'

'Mademoiselle, if it would give you pleasure, I shall make it my business to go and see Margot when I return to Saumur; and I shall let her know, in some way or other, that you are safe. '

'Thank you, Monsieur Michel, you are very good,' answered the little girl; 'you have taken a great weight off my mind. I shall now try to sleep, so as to be ready to proceed on our journey when it is time to do so. '

THE FUGITIVES ESCAPE

Whilst the fugitives are making their way to the coast, let us return to Etienne Simon's house. When his wife rose early in the morning, she looked out for her husband and son. Not seeing anything of them, she went back to the house, and busied herself about her usual occupations. As time wore on, she began to feel anxious at their non-appearance; going out again, and seeing old Marcel attending to the kiln, she went up and asked what he thought could have detained them; but she had trouble to make him understand, and when at last she succeeded, he only shook his head, and said, 'He did not know.'

Margot then thought of Suzanne; taking the ladder, she put it up in its usual place, and called out to her to make haste down. Receiving no answer, she called again and again, each time in a louder key than before, but always with the same result. She then resolved to go up to Suzanne's dormitory, to see what ailed the child; and having with great exertion clambered up, she commenced a search for her. To her utter astonishment she found the loft empty; every bundle of hay was turned over, and every corner of the place ransacked by her, but of course without success. What had become of Suzanne was beyond Margot's comprehension. She at once set down her disappearance to supernatural agency, and came to the conclusion that the child had been carried off by some being, not of human mould; and as this thought took possession, the poor old creature began invoking the blessed Virgin, and all the saints in the calendar, and imploring their aid in her present tribulation.

After wearying herself with looking for the little girl, she was just preparing to descend to the lower part of the building, when the thought flashed across her mind, that perhaps the unaccountable absence of her relatives might have some connection with the mysterious disappearance of the child. Her heart died within her when she remembered that Father Anselmo had so lately been there, and that perhaps it was by his orders that Suzanne had been carried away. She feared that Etienne and his son had been tempted by the priest to remove her secretly. The thought was agony; and she prayed that if such were the case, their great sin might be forgiven them.

Marguerite Simon really loved Suzanne. The child's uncomplaining patience had exercised a silent influence on the woman, and her better nature had reasserted itself. By degrees she had learnt to curb her temper, which had become hardened and soured by ill-usage. Less often was the angry retort heard; and she refrained from uttering taunts, which, though richly deserved both by her husband and son, never failed to infuriate them, and make them more savage in their demeanour than would otherwise have been the case; and, although the two men continued as unamiable and uncouth as before, there was more peace in the house.

Suzanne's habits of neatness had also manifested themselves

in the interior of the rude dwelling. There was a greater air of comfort than there had been heretofore, and altogether the poor woman had reason to lament the loss of her young companion; she had indeed 'been entertaining an angel unawares,' and she never forgot the child's sweet sad face, or her quiet, gentle manners to her dying day.

Hour after hour passed, and still absent ones did not return. Towards evening Margot heard the tramp of heavy footsteps, and looking out, she saw her husband and Mathurin approaching the house. She went hastily to inquire the cause of their protracted absence, but soon saw they were in no humour to be questioned; she therefore silently placed their supper before them, and after satisfying their appetites, they retired to rest, without even inquiring for Suzanne.

The next morning, however, Etienne called her as usual, and then his wife was obliged to tell him that she was nowhere to be found.

His fury knew no bounds. He accused his wife of having connived at her escape, and he used threats of all sorts to compel her to say where the child was gone. It was of no use for Margot to affirm that she knew nothing whatever of what had become of Suzanne; her husband was in no mood to listen, and he appealed to his son, whose rage was even more ungovernable than his own. At last, when the storm of passion had somewhat abated, they became more reasonable; and Margot then ventured to say, 'I wish I did know where the poor little girl is, for a great load would be taken off my mind; that dreadful Father Anselmo will be here again soon, and he will be so angry with us if we cannot give him a satisfactory account of the affair. Oh! I wish I did know where Suzanne is!'

The name of Father Anselmo struck terror into the hearts of the two men; they knew better than Margot what it was to oppose his will; and they eagerly consulted as to the best means of telling him.

Mathurin's advice was to let the matter rest until he came

again; which, he devoutly hoped would not be for a long time. His father and mother agreed with him, and they silently betook themselves to their usual occupations.

Father Anselmo did come, on the second day after their return; and when he found Suzanne de l'Orme had disappeared from Simon's house, his anger was terrible. He said they had conveyed her away on purpose, and he would make them pay dearly for what they had done. He affected to believe that they had taken pity on her, and carried her to some place where he could not have access to her; but, he added, as he lashed himself up to a state bordering on frenzy, 'you know the punishment inflicted on those who harbour or assist a Huguenot; and, before you are much older you shall rue the day when you thwarted my designs.'

'Huguenot, or no Huguenot,' exclaimed old Margot, 'that child is an angel upon earth, and well would it be for some of us who call ourselves Catholics if we were more like her. I, for one, rejoice if she has escaped; but I much fear she is not alive now – how could she have come down from that loft in the dark? This part of the country is quite unknown to her, and surely if she has wandered away from this place, she will have fallen into some pond or stream, and perhaps been drowned. 'And as this frightful conviction forced itself upon her mind, the poor woman wept aloud.

The priest was fairly puzzled, he did not know what to think; but his malevolent spirit did not give up all hope of recovering the prey which for the present had escaped; and he turned over in his mind the means of finding the little fugitive, although he had not the slightest clue as yet, which could lead to her discovery. As to her having disappeared through supernatural agency, as the simple Margot suggested, he of course scouted this idea; and he laughed her to scorn for even imagining such a thing. In his anger and vexation, he quite forgot the character he was in the habit of simulating, and let his true disposition appear. Instead of being a pious and affectionate teacher, whose only care was the salvation of souls, he showed such a vindictive spirit, and such a cruel determination to crush his little victim, that his hearers, rough and unlettered as they were, could not help observing his animosity, and commenting on it. Margot, whose mind had received a new impulse from the companionship of Suzanne, and had become desirous of leading a better life through her example, could not help telling Father Anselmo that she thought it was wrong to compel a child, by such harsh means, to abandon a religion, which after all, could not be so bad, if all who professed it were as pure and gentle as the little companion whose loss she deplored.

Father Anselmo looked at her contemptuously, and as he turned away, he hissed, rather than said, 'Woman, beware! You will find later what the penalty is for expressing such sentiments. I have only to say the word, and your doom is sealed!'

With these words he left the house and walked straight to the village where Monsieur de l'Orme and Victor had rested the memorable day on which Suzanne was found. He stopped to take some refreshment at the very auberge where they also had rested; curiously enough, he sat on the same seat as they had done, in front of the house, little dreaming who had occupied it so lately. It seemed strange that he did not proceed at once to the house of the venerable curé of the village; but he and that worthy man were so opposed in their opinions, that he did not care to meet him. One was a meek and gentle disciple of the Master whom he served, and his whole life was spent in doing good; whilst the other was bent on doing what seemed best to his depraved heart, without reference to the will of the Great Being whose minister he professed to be; and no motive of real religion actuated him, in any one of his schemes for making converts to his creed. No wonder, then, that he avoided coming in contact with his pious colleague, and that the hostelry had more attraction for him than the quiet home of the good curé.

Whilst he was taking the refreshment set before him, he made inquiries of the landlord whether anything extraordinary had occurred during the last few days; and on his replying in the negative, he asked, 'If they had seen any strangers lately?' At first, the landlord could not remember; but on being pressed more closely, he recollected that two men had been there two days before, and had remained a few hours. 'What were they like?' Was Father Anselmo's next question.

'They looked like farmers, but I did not notice them particularly. '

'Which way did they go?'

'I really did not observe' – and with this meagre information Father Anselmo was obliged to be content.

His brain, however, was soon at work, and he determined to unravel the mystery, 'coute qui coute. 'Having rested sufficiently, and paid his reckoning, he went his way, cogitating on the means he would employ to find Suzanne again.

Meanwhile the Simons were in great trepidation as to the result of the affair, and for once, old Etienne thought fit to consult his wife as to the best method of averting the wrath of the priest. Mathurin, not yet recovered from the effects of his expedition, was too sulky to say anything much to the purpose; and, after a few oaths and angry exclamations, he went back to his work in the brickfield.

Not so his father. The danger to which he imagined they were exposed, softened his natural churlishness, and he became so much more tractable, that his poor wife ventured on asking him, 'What had detained them so long at the fair?'

Etienne told her that having transacted the business which had taken them there, they had gone to an auberge, and having there met with some acquaintances, they had sat drinking together. Mathurin had been induced to take part in some gambling game: and having been cheated of his money, had, under the influence of drink, become very abusive; this was returned by his antagonist with interest, until from words they came to blows; and Mathurin (notwithstanding his height and strength) got the worst of it. He was knocked down, and for some time remained insensible. Etienne meanwhile stayed to watch over him. When Mathurin recovered his senses, he was too much stunned to resume the journey; they therefore decided on remaining where they were until the next day, when they returned home, tired and crest-fallen at the result of their expedition.

'And what have you done with the dogs, Etienne?'

'The dogs!' he questioned, as if remembering them for the first time.

'Yes, the dogs!'

'Oh, I had forgotten the poor beasts; they followed us the morning we left, and that did not please Mathurin. He tried to send them back, but when they would persist in coming on in spite of him, he became so furious, that he gave a violent kick to poor Hector, which sent it spinning into a ditch, where he lay moaning and howling for a few minutes, and then all was still – the poor brute was dead. I was very sorry, and I gave it well to Mathurin; but what was the use? It could not bring the dog back to life. '

'No, indeed!' said Margot, sighing: 'Poor old Hector, I am so sorry for him. But where is César?'

'I am sure I don't know; we quite lost sight of him. '

At this moment a scratching noise was heard against the door, and a low whine announced the return of the truant. Margot opened the door at once, and the poor dog dragged himself into the kitchen, and lay down at his master's feet, wagging his tail, as if to show his pleasure at being once more at home. Notwithstanding the blows and kicks he was in the habit of receiving, the poor animal's fidelity was unshaken. He looked thin and half-starved, and a fragment of rope round his neck showed that he had been detained against his will.

Providence had overruled all. The dogs, which would have proved an insuperable hindrance to Monsieur de l'Orme's plan for removing Suzanne, had been kept away until their return could not be of any consequence one way or the other.

In the meantime, Father Anselmo was making his way back

to Saumur, and during his walk thither, he decided on going at once to the 'Maire' of the town, and securing his co-operation in recovering the fugitive. That important functionary willingly agreed to give all the help in his power; at the same time asking many questions as to the direction which ought to be taken in making the search. Here we shall leave them for the present, and devote the next chapter to the travellers, and what befell them.

TOWARDS THE COAST

Whilst the 'Maire' and the priest were deliberating on the important subject we have described in the foregoing chapter, Monsieur de l'Orme and his party were steadily advancing towards the coast. Their progress was slow, for Suzanne's strength seemed to decrease each day, and she was almost incapable of bearing the motion of being carried. Once she became so faint and ill, that her friends were quite alarmed about her; and Victor, regardless of consequences, rushed about seeking if perchance he might find some charitable being who could give them assistance. Happily he was guided to a charcoal burner's hut, and he no sooner made known his wishes, than he was supplied with goat's milk wherewith to refresh the poor exhausted wanderer. These kind-hearted people did not stop to consider whether there might be any difference in their creed, but they cheerfully gave what they could; and poor

Suzanne was very grateful for the refreshing draught. It enabled her to bear up for a little longer, and her father whispered to her to be of good courage, as their journey was drawing to an end.

Suzanne smiled faintly, as she replied in a low voice, 'Do you think, dear father, that I shall live to see my mother again, and Marthe, and the little ones?'

Pierre de l'Orme turned his head away, and for some moments could not reply. In his own mind he did not think there was a chance of it; but he answered as calmly as he could, 'My daughter, with God all things are possible, and it may please Him to restore your strength ere long – trust in Him, my child, and all will yet be well. '

Suzanne was comforted, and assured her father that she was ready to submit to anything it might please God to order for her. He then pressed her to try to take some repose, which she did, and when she awoke they resumed their journey.

They were now approaching the road again. The trees no longer grew so thickly, or in such long continuous lines. Large cleared spaces began to be more frequent, and Monsieur de l'Orme rejoiced, for his child's sake, that they would soon be on open ground again. It was late in the afternoon when they arrived on the confines of the forest. The day had been an unusually sultry one, and there was a heaviness in the atmosphere, which denoted the approach of a thunder-storm. Not a breath of air stirred the trees overhead, and although they afforded shade from the scorching rays of the sun, the tired wanderers found it hardly possible to breathe. Suzanne was so weak and weary that she could no longer sit behind her father, and consequently he was obliged to hold her in his arms, as he best could. They went on slowly; and before emerging in to the high road, it was thought advisable that they should stop whilst Victor went forward to reconnoitre, and make sure it was safe for them to proceed. It was well he did so, and the sequel will show.

Before he ventured out of the shelter of the trees and brushwood he looked about him cautiously; and, coming from the direction they were about to follow, he saw a party of horsemen approaching. Not knowing whether they were friends or foes, he wisely determined to keep out of sight until they had gone by. He accordingly crept under some bushes (he had left his horse with his companions) and remained perfectly still, scarcely daring even to breathe.

On they came. By the clanking of their sabres, and their warlike accoutrements, he knew they must be soldiers, and if so, they were on no peaceful errand.

Victor's terror may be more easily conceived than described, when he heard their leader call out to them to halt; and they did so, not many paces from his place of concealment. Could any of his friends have seen Victor le Grand's face then, they would hardly have recognised it. Every trace of colour had left his usually ruddy countenance, and he shook like an aspen, at the danger which they were at that moment incurring. He was a brave man, or he would not have volunteered to share the perils which Monsieur de l'Orme had to go through; but when he thought of the helpless child, and her devoted father, who were so soon perhaps, to be taken captive, after so nearly effecting their escape, his heart almost fainted within him. There was no help for it, however, and he determined to await the issue of this new danger.

'What atrocious heat!' were the first words which fell on his ear.

'Aye, you may well say so; one feels grilled alive, and I wish Monsieur le Maire would not choose the dog days for hunting the Huguenots,' remarked another of the soldiers.

'The dog days! Why, you don't suppose these are the dog days yet, do you, Jules? However, the heat is quite enough to make one think so, and I do wish Monsieur d'Aureville would let us go into the forest, and ride under the shade of the trees, I am sure it would be cooler.'

'You matter of fact old stupid! Who stops to consider whether one is right or wrong in such weather – for my part I wish we were safe at Saumur again; besides, I am not so sure you are right either, although you pretend to be so much wiser than your neighbours; but look at that abominable long dusty road; not a tree for miles, I'll wager; it makes one thirsty to look at it. '

'Never mind, Jules; there will be an end to it, as well as to everything else; and we certainly would be much longer going through the forest than by the road, hot and dusty though it be. '

'Ha! Ha! Look at Jacques Moulin, he does not seem to like it better than any of us,' laughed Jules.

'Well, I don't suppose you would, either, in his place,' interposed a quiet-looking man; 'only think if your wedding had been put off to go on this wild goose chase. I hardly think you would have been very merry over it, would you? Don't mind them, my lad,' he added, turning to the young man who looked somewhat chafed at their banter, and who had begun a warm reply to it.

There was a chance of a quarrel arising, when a loud authoritative voice was heard inquiring what was the matter? On understanding it was something which concerned Moulin, the leader of the band called him up; and giving the order to move on, he desired him to give an account of what had just passed.

The young man, flattered by the notice of his commanding officer, proceeded to tell him that his marriage, which was to have taken place a few days before, had been put a stop to by the expedition they were now engaged in; and that he had with difficulty obtained leave to go and tell his 'fiancée' of the change which it was necessary to make; 'and now,' he added despondingly, 'who knows when it will be able to take place, for we may be sent in twenty different directions on this senseless business. '

'I shall attend to that,' replied Monsieur d'Aureville; 'but beware, my good lad, that you are not overheard when you make such speeches as the last. I can make every allowance for your disappointment; but there are some,' – and he glanced back at his followers – 'who would only be too glad to give information that you have a kindly feeling towards the Huguenots; and thereby, get into favour with those who hate and persecute them. Take care of Meunier,' he went on, lowering his voice; 'I fear he is concocting mischief; he is a great deal too silent; there is a look in his eye which bodes no good. '

'Thank you, Monsieur, I shall be cautious,' answered the young man.

Monsieur d'Aureville then proceeded to ask him where his intended bride lived, so that when making application for his leave, he might know what length of time to request.

Jacques Moulin replied, 'Perhaps Monsieur may remember the inn at that place kept by Picard? It is his youngest daughter I am about to marry. When I was there a few days ago, they were all in a commotion at the mysterious disappearance of a little girl who lived at Simons, the brickmakers, whose house is about half a mile farther than the village. This girl, up to the present time, has passed as their grandchild; but, there seems to be some doubt about that now. My little Marie was quite excited about it, for it seems she saw the child not long ago; and noticing how ill and sad she looked, she spoke to the old man about it. Marie had occasion to go there on some errand for her father, and she says she never can forget what she witnessed. Can you fancy, Monsieur, a child, apparently not more than twelve years of age, carrying a load of bricks on a hand barrow with a man six feet high?'

'Impossible!' exclaimed the officer.

'No, Monsieur, I assure you it is true; and Marie spoke to the old man on the subject. He was very rude and churlish and told her he had a right to do as he pleased, and nobody need meddle. Marie, nothing daunted, asked who the little girl belonged to ,and he gave her to understand that she was the child of his daughter Victoire, who married some years ago, and sent to live in a distant town; that her parents were both dead, and that she had been sent to them, and he added, 'I can't afford to keep

113

her doing nothing, so she must work. ' He then turned away, so Marie was obliged to leave the subject. It seems that this is the tale which has been told to whoever made any inquiry about the child; but as few persons ever took the trouble of doing so – the Simons not being people whose acquaintance was much sought, as their character is not of the best – the subject had been almost forgotten. Now it seems this tale was an untruth, and that the child we are sent in search of, is the one whom Marie saw. '

'This is all very strange,' said Monsieur d'Aureville, 'but we cannot go back from our duty, Moulin, much as we may dislike it; however, return to your place now, and be discreet. I fear a storm is brewing.' As he said the words, a flash of lightning illuminated the darkening sky, and a loud peal of thunder showed that it might be nearer than even he had expected. Giving the word to go forward, he set spurs to his horse, an example which was at once followed by his men.

For some time they rode on in silence; and the storm increasing every moment, they went at a rapid pace. A flash of lightning of intense vividness, followed by a deafening crash, startled the horse of one of the soldiers; it reared suddenly, and the man, appalled probably by the sound of the thunder, which echoed and re-echoed for many seconds, was thrown off his guard, and fell heavily to the ground, where he lay stunned and senseless, while his frightened charger galloped off at a speed which defied pursuit.

The prostrate man's comrades at once dismounted; and finding him unable to move, they by Monsieur d'Aureville's order, carried him to a farm-house at a little distance from where the accident had happened. Here they stayed a short time to restore him; but being unable to do so, it was decided that the party should ride on, one of them being left to assist the farm people in trying to bring back the sufferer to consciousness. Monsieur d'Aureville, having ascertained that the man was only stunned, and would most probably recover his senses ere long, was unwilling to delay longer; he had reasons for doing so. The man who was hurt was Meunier, against whom he had cautioned Jacques Moulin during their conversation; and was therefore not sorry to have the opportunity of reaching Saumur before him, and he had many things to do which that man's meddling might mar.

A LONG JOURNEY

Monsieur d'Aureville was a Roman Catholic, and a good man, loyal to his king and country, but his soul revolted at the atrocities which were perpetrated in the name of religion, and with the approval of the higher powers. He, in common with thousands professing his creed, deplored the persecution of their Huguenot brethren, and did all in his power to mitigate the severity of the orders which he dared not disobey.

Of an ancient and noble family, whose name was proverbial for chivalry and integrity, he had, from his earliest years, been brought up to the profession of arms; and as soon as he was of an age to do so, had entered the army. Although a young man still, he had done good service in the field, as more than one scar could testify. But although Armand d'Aureville was a brave and distinguished officer, and the possessor of many virtues, together with great personal advantages, still there was one thing he lacked, and that was blind subserviency to the wishes and caprices of 'Le Grand Monarque,' and those who instigated him in his injustices towards the Protestant portion of his subjects. Consequently he had never risen to any very high grade in the service, and was still less likely to do so now; for with all his prudence, he could not quite disguise his aversion and repugnance to the work he had now been engaged upon for some time past; that is to say, hunting out the poor unoffending Huguenots, and dragging them to prison, and often to death. However, he well knew the risk he incurred, when he slurred over his orders, and was generally cautious in his way of acting.

His first care, on his return to Saumur, was to obtain Jacques Moulin's leave of absence. He had a fellow-feeling with him, being himself engaged to a young lady, to whom he was much attached, and his marriage was only delayed by the unsettled state of the times. From his fiancée, Berthe d'Aubigny – whose father, an eminent lawyer, had a secret leaning towards the Reformed faith, although he had not yet declared it – Armand d'Aureville had learned to look leniently upon their supposed heretical tenets; and the time was not far distant when he too, would be called upon to give up home and country for the sake of the religion which he learned to profess and love. The persecutions which the Huguenots were subjected to – the tyrannical measures which were adopted, to force them to renounce the opinions in which they had been brought up – were hateful to him; and as time went on his disgust increased. Thousands of children were torn from their parents, to be educated in convents, and very few ever saw their homes or friends again. Suzanne de l'Orme was one of those few; but even her rescue was not effected, until months of suffering had elapsed.

Monsieur d'Aureville knew of these iniquitous proceedings; and this, more than anything else, tended to make him doubt the genuineness of a religion whose appointed professors could so cruelly outrage the laws of humanity. He thought it the height of injustice to separate children from their natural protectors on such grounds, and accordingly, when he received orders to hunt out Suzanne, although he did not know the exact nature of her case, he yet determined not to go out of his way to find her. He would obey to a certain point, but beyond that no power on earth should make him go.

He heard perfectly well when his men expressed a wish to ride through the forest; but, as he thought it very likely that it might be chosen as a hiding-place by any person wishing to escape, he entirely ignored their wishes, and thus enabled our fugitives to remain unmolested.

When he arrived at Saumur, he of course reported his want of success. His account, as it happened, met with little attention, for, during his absence, events of greater importance had occurred; and even Father Anselmo was consoled for the loss of his intended victim, by the prospect of greater triumphs.

Huguenot meetings had taken place in various parts of the country; and as these meetings were contrary to the then established laws of France, Monsieur d'Aureville was despatched, with the men under his command to a distant province; and it was not until years afterwards, when he, with his wife and family, had effected their escape to England, that he heard how nearly he had been the means of ruining Monsieur de l'Orme's efforts to rescue his daughter. His orders were to go to Paimbœf in search of the child, and to Paimbœf he had gone. Having found nothing there to excite suspicion, he returned at once, turning neither to the right or to the left. He had no command to do so; and although the shade of the trees would have been most grateful on that sultry afternoon, he would not avail himself of it.

Whilst we have been following Monsieur d'Aureville to Saumur, Victor le Grand had returned to his friends. They were struck with the pallor of his countenance, and eagerly questioned him as to what had happened to disturb him. He told them in a few words what had occurred. Their emotion was only exceeded by the extreme thankfulness which they felt at this unlooked-

119

for deliverance, and on their knees they thanked their Almighty Protector.

They then remounted, and Victor leading the way, they once more emerged into the road. It was high time they did so. The sky was becoming more and more overcast, and the muttering of distant thunder was heard more frequently. Victor urged as much speed as possible, for he foresaw that a storm of more than common fury was impending. Monsieur de l'Orme and Jacques Michel, knowing too the necessity there was for haste, increased the pace of their horses as much as Suzanne's feeble state allowed. It was not long before the tempest broke out. Flash followed flash in constant succession, and the thunder waxed louder and louder; large drops of rain began to fall on the heated road, and it soon descended in torrents on the unprotected travellers.

Victor le Grand suggested the propriety of his riding on to apprise his brother and sister of their approach, and to get everything ready for their reception; an offer which was gratefully accepted, as the rest of the party knew their way sufficiently to proceed without his guidance. This point settled, he spurred on his horse, and was soon out of sight.

As the storm increased, Pierre de l'Orme blessed God that they had left the dangerous shelter of the forest, and kept up his little daughter's courage with words of endearment and comfort. He wrapped her up in his cloak, and thus protected her from the deluge which was now pouring down upon them.

As they approached the coast they could distinctly hear the roaring of the sea; and this sound, mingled with the crashing of thunder overhead, was listened to with awe, not unmixed with alarm, by the tired wanderers, all unused as they were to hear the noise of the vast deep, when its depths are stirred from quietude and repose, by the word of Him who is Lord of all!

At length they reached the spot where, scarcely a year before, Monsieur de l'Orme and his family had halted, to give their friends warning of their arrival. There was no need to stop now, and the anxious father and his kind-hearted companion hailed with joy the sight of the foaming ocean; for they knew that shelter was at hand, and that their little exhausted charge would soon find a resting-place, with friends who would take every care of her.

As they neared the shore, the sight which presented itself to them was far different from what Pierre de l'Orme had witnessed on a former occasion. The sea *then* was like a mirror, reflecting every passing cloud, and dazzlingly beautiful in the sparkling sunlight – *now*, the angry waves came dashing up, lashing each other in their fury, and thundering on the shingle in constant succession and awful grandeur. It was a scene of intense sublimity, and none but the most hardened could witness it without emotion. The little party, now exposed to the pitiless tempest, felt that the voice of God was in the storm, and with bowed heads they acknowledged His power.

Through the blinding rain they pressed on, and at length arrived at le Grand's cottage. There, as before, Jeanne stood on the threshold to receive them, and warm was her greeting: but tears gathered in her mild blue eyes, and slowly rolled down her face, when she gazed on the helpless being whom she had taken from her father's arms into her own. She immediately took her upstairs, and, while the others were divesting themselves of their dripping garments, she put the poor worn-out child to bed. She then went down to get some strengthening broth, which was in readiness against their arrival: this revived poor little Suzanne wonderfully, and, grateful for the kindness shown to her, she murmured prayers for her kind friends, and in doing so fell asleep, utterly regardless of the conflict of the elements raging without.

She slept for some hours – a sleep so sound as almost to resemble that of death. Tired nature was exhausted, and finding herself once more in a clean, comfortable bed, Suzanne yielded to the drowsy feeling which came over her, unable, as well as unwilling, to do battle against it. Jeanne le Grand having satisfied herself that she would want nothing until she woke again, went down to attend to her other guests, and to hear and relate all that had happened during the absence of Monsieur de l'Orme and her brother Victor.

The meeting between Jacques Michel and his niece was one which afforded them great pleasure, for they had not seen each other for a long time, and they had much to talk about. There were, however, events of much greater moment than ordinary family affairs, to enlarge upon; and her hearers were astonished at the information which Jeanne gave them. Victor having arrived before the others, had gleaned a few particulars; but his sister had been too busy, preparing for the reception of her guests, to be able to talk much; he therefore gladly joined the listeners, and the recital of their own adventures was deferred till a later period.

Paul le Grand not having yet appeared, the cause of his absence was asked; and then his sister told them he was gone to Paimbœf to make arrangements with the captain of their vessel to convey all the family to England, it being no longer safe for them to remain in their native land, and they were only waiting for the return of Victor and his friends to take their departure. Not having heard of Suzanne's discovery, they had not dared to hope she would have been of the party; but now there was no drawback to their leaving, except parting with their beloved uncle.

Jacques Michel was surprised at this news, but not so much so as might have been expected. In those times, promptitude of action was often necessary to secure life and property; and none knew when their turn would come to share the exile's fate. He was grieved and saddened to part with the last remnant of his family; but he soon cheered up, and said, 'Who knows how soon my good wife and I shall follow; we shall perhaps pay you a visit ere long. '

Jeanne and her brother brightened up at this remark and she resumed her account of what had taken place during the last few weeks.

Whilst Monsieur de l'Orme had been prosecuting his search for Suzanne, rumours had reached the Protestants at Paimbœf and its environs, that extreme measures of harshness had been used towards the members of the Reformed Church in many places. Some of the Huguenots, with more zeal than judgment, had persisted in assembling together at times when it was madness to do so. Others had been hot-headed enough to resist the soldiers who had been sent to disperse or apprehend them; and having been found with weapons on their persons, in direct infraction of the law then in force, scenes of violence and bloodshed had been the result.

Paul le Grand and his sister, tired of living in a state of perpetual alarm and discomfort, had come to the conclusion that it would be wiser to leave France before worse times came; and as they had no near relatives but their uncle and his wife, their decision was less painful than it would otherwise have been. They also had the hope of one day being able to return to the home endeared to them by early association — and so it was decided. They did not wait for Victor's sanction, for they knew that where they went he would follow; and even now Paul was gone to the seaport to carry some of the things which they wished to take with them. They did not possess many valuables; but there were several little relics, which would remind them of the home they were leaving, when they were exiles in a foreign land.

Wishing to avoid comment and suspicion, they had, a little by degrees, parted with their farm implements and domestic animals, and had thus amassed sufficient money to enable them to prosecute the journey they were about to undertake. Their household furniture they were obliged to leave behind. This grieved poor Jeanne sorely; but she bore up bravely for the sake of her brothers, and was full of courage and resolution.

Whilst she was relating the foregoing details to her attentive listeners, the storm continued raging with unabated fury. The thunder resembled the roar of artillery, and the lightning flashes were of a vividness awful to behold. Victor was with difficulty withheld from rushing out to meet his brother, who, he felt persuaded, must be in the midst of it; but Jeanne and his friends represented to him that it was next to an impossibility that this should be the case, for the storm must have commenced ere he could have left Paimbœf, and no one in his senses would have ventured on leaving a place of shelter in such weather. He was convinced, and yielded to their wishes and advice.

Meanwhile Jeanne le Grand had not been idle. Her active hands had prepared a substantial meal for her half-famished guests, who did ample justice to what she had provided for them. There was the nourishing 'pottage' or soup, which no well-ordered housekeeper in France is ever without. Roast fowls – a savoury 'omelette' – salad, and fish fresh caught from the neighbouring sea, completed the entertainment, with the addition of good wholesome bread, and a bottle or two of the ordinary 'Vin du pays,' which is the usual beverage of the inhabitants of that part of France. They were hungry men before whom these appetizing foods were placed; but their appetites being at last satisfied, Jeanne cleared the table of the relics of the feast, and was soon occupied in a different manner. Some of her garments were brought out, and she set to work to cut them down, so as to fit Suzanne in lieu of the soiled and ragged ones she had been clothed in. Such was her industry, that ere many hours had elapsed, she had everything ready for the child to put on.

Night had now closed in, and gradually the storm decreased. The thunder was no longer so incessant or so loud, and there was a prospect of a calmer night than might have been expected. Some of the party began to show signs of fatigue; and it was determined that they should retire to rest early, with the exception of Jeanne, who would sit up for her brother. Jacques Michel, who had announced his intention of returning home the next morning, was at first unwilling to do so without seeing his eldest nephew; but the good man was so completely worn out by the exertions of the last few days, that he also agreed to the decision of the others, on the condition that Jeanne should awaken him if Paul arrived, and he wished to have some conversation with him before separating, perhaps for ever. Jeanne promised, and then the assembled family knelt down, and, after their custom, asked the Divine protection on themselves and their absent kindred.

Before they retired for the night, they went to take a look at the little sleeper upstairs, for whose sake they had all incurred such risks, and who, by the sweetness of her disposition, had won the love and affection of all. She had not moved from the position in which she had been placed; and the soft regularity of her breathing showed how calmly and peacefully she was resting. As they gazed on her attenuated features, and the transparent delicacy of her complexion, they felt she was hovering on the confines of another world, and that nothing short of a miracle of God's goodness could restore her to health and strength.

As the Huguenot looked on his child, thoughts of unutterable sadness crowded on his mind; he foresaw the grief of his poor Madeleine if he arrived without their beloved daughter, and according to present appearances it was hardly probable she would live through the voyage to England. At the thought of such a possibility, the unhappy father's fortitude almost gave way; but Jeanne, seeing what was passing in his mind, with womanly sympathy, insisted on their leaving the room, and retiring to the resting-places prepared for them.

The storm was now nearly over; and about two hours afterwards, the sound of a horse's hoofs were heard. In an instant the animal had stopped and the well-known signal of her brothers, when they were obliged to remain away from home late, having been given, Jeanne opened the door. Paul led his horse to the stable; and having attended to him, he entered the house. He looked tired and harassed; but, on being told of the arrival of Victor and his companions, he uttered an exclamation of joy and thankfulness.

'Heaven be praised, Jeanne! Our way is clear now. I have been very anxious on their account, for a party of soldiers has been to Paimbœf making inquiries about Huguenot fugitives; and, from what I could learn, they were in search of Mademoiselle de l'Orme. Happily they were commanded by an officer who is friendly to our cause, otherwise the consequences of their visit might have been serious, not only to our good friends, but to themselves. They did not remain long, but went back to Saumur, to report their want of success. '

Jeanne le Grand's consternation was great at the news she heard; she felt, as well as her brother, that the fugitives had narrowly escaped being captured. She then told Paul of her uncle's visit to them, and of the circumstances which had occasioned it; and it was decided that, as soon as it was light, she should rouse them both, so that they might have a few hours to themselves before he returned homewards. They then separated for the night, but not before Paul had told his sister that the vessel would be round the point the next evening, unless another storm should come on, when they would be compelled to defer their embarkation. He, however, thought there was no chance of such a thing, as the night promised to be fine, and the sky was no longer heavy with clouds, as it had been for the two or three previous days.

For a few hours all was silent in the farm-house; nought was heard but the heavy surging of the restless waves; and the dwellers in that house slept as calmly and profoundly as if no danger hovered over them. The returning day, however, once more recalled the sleepers to a sense of their precarious position; and they were ere long up, and busy making the necessary preparations for their voyage. Jeanne, with her usual care, having prepared a good store of provisions, these were packed in large hampers and baskets; and as Jacques Michel had been prevailed upon to remain with them until they embarked in the evening, he busied himself with Paul and Victor in conveying them to the vessel.

This proceeding excited no surprise at Paimbœf, as the brothers were in the habit of carrying the produce of their farm to the market there; and they therefore accomplished their journeys to and fro without question.

When Suzanne awoke, she felt much refreshed. Jeanne gave her some breakfast, and then helped her to dress, after which she sat by the open window enjoying the invigorating sea breeze, and looking on with amusement at the strange scene before her. The sea was still somewhat agitated, and the waves rolled in heavily; but the sun shone brightly, and there was the prospect of fine weather for their voyage. Her father came to see how she felt after her night's rest, and was comforted to observe the improvement in her looks. He spoke hopefully of their journey, and said, 'that although the sea was not very calm, he hoped it would soon be more so,' and added, 'you will not be afraid, my Suzanne, when you are on the great ocean, if the vessel rolls and tosses? You know we may not always have fine weather, and it may please God to send us storms before we reach England. '

'Yes, Father, I know; but why should we fear? He is able to protect us on the sea as well as on the land. Yesterday we were exposed to as fearful a tempest as I think it is possible to be in, and yet we were mercifully preserved. When I was so often alone, and sad, and weary, I used to think of all the beautiful Scripture stories which good Monsieur Morin told me and the children, when he came to see us. I remember well the one which relates to the storm, when our Saviour was asleep in the little vessel with His disciples, when He rebuked the wind and the waves, and they were safe, although they had been in such fear and peril. Do you not think, my father, that He would do the same for us, if we prayed to Him earnestly?'

'Most certainly, my child!' and for the second time Monsieur de l'Orme felt that his faith had fallen short of that which animated the spirit of a being so much weaker than himself. They conversed for some time longer, and at length he left Suzanne full of hope that they would have a prosperous journey, and a happy meeting with all their beloved ones.

The day at length came to an end; and when darkness had set

in, the little party issued from the house in silence. They could not speak, for their hearts were too full of sadness for words – at least those of the le Grands and their uncle. Monsieur de l'Orme and Suzanne respected their sorrow: their own was light by comparison, for they were going to the home they had already made for themselves in England, whilst their friends were leaving theirs for the first time, and perhaps for ever.

Sad was the leave-taking, but at last it was over, and Suzanne was laid tenderly on a mattress provided for her accommodation by the thoughtful kindness of her friend Jeanne, and which had been placed in the bottom of the boat. Before quitting the house, she had again reminded Jacques Michel of his promise to see and comfort old Margot; and he had again assured her that it should be as she wished, if it were at all in his power. He also promised Monsieur de l'Orme to use his utmost endeavours to find out what had become of Monsieur Morin, and to let him know the result of his inquiries as soon as he had the opportunity.

And so they parted.

Jacques Michel returned to his home full of apprehension for the future, and resolved, if possible, to leave a country which was day by day becoming more and more unsafe for those of his persuasion.

Whilst he was journeying homewards, the boat was making slow progress, for it was heavily laden, but at last the ship was reached, and with some difficulty all were safely got on board. The last package had just been hauled up, when shouts were heard on the shore, and through the stillness of the night the splash of oars was heard.

'We are pursued!' exclaimed the captain. 'Look sharp, my men! We must not allow ourselves to be captured. '

The sailors worked with a will; but notwithstanding their exertions, the boat gained on them, and the shout 'De par le Roi,' was distinctly heard by all on board. To the terrified refugees the sound was like the knell of departing hopes, and they gave up all for lost, for by the faint light they could see that the boat in chase was filled with armed men. Capitaine la Croix enjoined the strictest silence; and having distributed arms to his crew and passengers, he told them, in a low voice, to be ready to fire the moment he gave the word to do so. On, on came the pursuers, and they were now so near that their different voices could be distinguished one from the other. Again was the captain commanded in the king's name to stop, but receiving no response, the citation was followed by shots, happily at random. From the motion of the boat, as it danced on the waves, it was not possible for the soldiers to take proper aim, and thus no one was hurt, with the exception of one of the sailors, whose cheek was grazed by one of the bullets, as it whizzed past the place where he was standing. It was only a slight wound, but it roused the spirit of his messmates; and when Capitaine la Croix thundered forth the word to fire, his men were only too glad to obey him. A well-directed volley was sent amongst the assailants, and their groans and shrieks announced the deadly effect it had. All seemed disorder and confusion in the boat. The sailors re-loaded their pieces, and waited their captain's orders to discharge them a second time at the unhappy wretches, who, after all, were only obeying the commands of those in authority over them. Several must have been killed and wounded, for none of the party attempted to fire again. Meanwhile the wind, which had only till now made the sails flap idly against the rigging of the vessel, all at once sprang up, and filled them out, and the 'Croix Blanche,' by a sudden impetus, glided swiftly onwards, and in a short time was beyond the reach of the danger. Fainter and still more faint, the cries of the wounded and the shouts of their incensed comrades, were borne on the breeze, and ere long the exiles felt they were saved.

'Ah!' exclaimed Capitaine le Croix, 'this is my last voyage in these parts for some time, I expect. I am sorry; but it cannot be helped. France will lose many of her children, if our king persists in his cruel and arbitrary proceedings; for, after all, it is better to expatriate one's self, than to live in a continual dread of death or imprisonment; and I, for one, am tired of it. '

This sentiment was echoed by all on board; and with deep thankfulness for the deliverance they had just now experienced, from the imminent peril which had threatened them, was mingled the hope, that a brighter future was in store for them, in the land to which they were proceeding.

How came it to pass that their flight was discovered, some of them never knew; and it was only when Monsieur de l'Orme met Armand d'Aureville, years afterwards, in London, that he learned to whom they were indebted for the information which had been conveyed to the authorities of Paimbœf, and which had led to their pursuit on the memorable night which has been described in the last chapter. It was Meunier who was the informer. It will be remembered that this Meunier was the man who was thrown from his horse during the fearful thunderstorm which raged on the day when Suzanne de l'Orme and her friends arrived at the le Grands abode, and of whom Monsieur d'Aureville was so suspicious. He was an artful scheming man, who suspected mischief in every trifling circumstance; and as he had been engaged in a great many expeditions of the kind, and almost always with persons less scrupulous than his present commanding officer, he had acquired a sort of relish for the employment, and prided himself on the sagacity with which he found out, and followed up the track of his persecuted fellow-subjects. Meunier did not exactly know who the fugitives were, but he suspected that the child whom he and his party were in search of, was not alone; and, in his wisdom, he came to the conclusion, that if one or more of the Huguenots, who in all probability accompanied her, were captured also through his exertions and instrumentality, it would be a good day's work for him; and bright visions of reward floated before his brain. It had not escaped his penetration, that Monsieur d'Aureville's inquiries had been very superficial – but he said nothing. He waited for a good opportunity to lay the imagined shortcomings of his chief before those who would be only too glad of any fault, however trivial, to bring him to account – and leniency to the Reformers was considered in the light of a crime of the blackest die, in the eyes of those who were determined to effect their ruin. What an easy task, then, for any one of Meunier's disposition, - one always plotting mischief, and seeking the destruction of others, however unoffending they might be, - to bring an accusation against a person already suspected of favouring the poor persecuted Protestants; for it needed very little additional testimony to convince the unjust judges of the guilt of the accused.

When Meunier recovered his senses after the accident, his thoughts reverted at once to what had previously taken place. He felt more and more convinced, that Monsieur d'Aureville had negligently performed the duty he had been sent upon; and he determined to make up for it himself, and at the same time pay out his superior officer, against whom he had for a long time a grudge. Accordingly, when his comrade proposed that they should proceed to Saumur, Meunier pleaded the loss of his horse, and saying he must make inquiries as to whether it had been caught in the neighbourhood, promised to follow as soon as he could. The other man, who was a heavy, stupid individual, not overburdened with brains, agreed to Meunier's proposal, and left him at the farm, quite regardless of what the consequences might be. This was just what the other wanted; and as soon as he could, he made up his mind to find his way back to Paimbœf, and there watch and wait, if need be, to see if his suspicions were correct. At the same time, he resolved to consult the authorities there, and ask their help.

Planning and doing are, however, two different things; when Meunier attempted to walk he found that he was not capable of carrying out what he intended, and was obliged, 'malgré lui,' to remain the night at the farm. He slept soundly, so soundly, that he did not wake until the morning was far advanced; and when he did so, he felt so dizzy and uncomfortable, that he could not begin his march until the afternoon. The farmer's wife gave him some food, and at length he set off upon his cruel errand. He could not walk fast, however; the roads were heavy after the torrents of rain which had fallen; and encumbered as he was with his enormous riding-boots, he found the journey anything but pleasant. Being almost always in the saddle, he was soon tired; and had not his love of mischief and his hatred of the Huguenots been paramount, he would have retraced his steps before he had accomplished half of the journey. As it was, he would not give in, and continued his weary walk.

It was late when he reached his destination, and then he had to find out those, without whose help he was powerless.

Capitaine la Croix had meanwhile taken his vessel quietly out of the harbour, and made his way to the spot where he was to receive his passengers; and by the time the necessary information was given and received, and the officials ready for action, the prey was beyond reach; Meunier was foiled. He never knew who had escaped, and was obliged to return to his legitimate duty, and to submit not only to reprimand but to punishment for his prolonged absence; a circumstance which did not tend to improve his feelings towards either the Huguenots or Monsieur d'Aureville.

JACQUES MICHEL

Whilst the exiles were proceeding to their place of refuge in England, Jacques Michel hastened on his homeward journey. He was anxious to return to his wife, having left her unprotected, and entertained some fears for her safety. On his arrival, he found her well, but in an agony of terror, not only about himself, but about the dreadful things which were happening to the Protestants all over the kingdom. Wicked men had been spreading all manner of false reports about the unhappy professors of that creed. The consequence was, that the ignorant and bigoted masses of the people, incited by such men as Father Anselmo, greedily devoured these idle tales, and committed all manner of outrages on their defenceless brethren openly, and with the sanction of those in authority.

As yet none of the atrocities which were being perpetrated in other parts of France had been enacted at Saumur, that town having been one of the principal strongholds of Calvinism; and the members of that faith mustering there in great numbers, their enemies, feared an outbreak, which might be inconvenient, if not difficult to quell; they waited until flight and expatriation had thinned the ranks of its stern and uncompromising upholders, before proceeding to extremities in that quarter. The time was not, however, far distant, when its Huguenot inhabitants would be called upon to suffer the same indignities as their unfortunate co-religionists.

Jacques Michel therefore told his wife that he had come to the determination of leaving France as soon as possible; and bade her make all necessary preparations for removal. Above all things he enjoined the strictest secrecy, for on that, safety depended. He then mentioned his promise to try to see old Margot, and as a means of doing so, he proposed going the following morning with his cart to fetch a load of bricks, for the ostensible reason of repairing his mill. He accordingly set out at an early hour, and in due time arrived at Simon's house. Having transacted the business for which he had come there, Jacques pleased fatigue, and asked to be allowed to rest a little while. Simon gave an ungracious assent, and added, that he was busy, so Monsieur Michel must content himself with his wife's society, as he had not time to waste on visitors.

This was just what honest Jacques wanted; he had not the slightest intention of letting old Simon or his son know the real reason of his errand; he knew their character sufficiently to be aware that they would at once denounce him as an assistant in Suzanne's escape; and being a Huguenot himself, albeit a useful one to the community at large, he would fare badly, if once cited before the prejudiced tribunal of Saumur.

When he entered the living-room or kitchen, he found Marguerite Simon sitting on a low seat by the open window. She was much altered, and seemed to have lost all energy, as the disorder and untidiness of the room plainly showed.

From the time of Suzanne de l'Orme's unaccountable

disappearance, the poor woman had not had a moment's peace; and she had pined away, as much from sorrow at the loss of the child, as from anxiety with regard to her safety.

Margot scarcely raised her head when Jacques Michel entered; and, but slightly noticed the hearty good-humoured 'bon jour,' with which he greeted her. He sat down on a bench opposite to her, and by degrees attracted her attention; then in a low voice he imparted Suzanne's message, and begged her in the name of the child to cease fretting on her account; she was happy with her father, and in the prospect of soon joining her mother and the rest of the family; and, he added, 'she told me to say to you, that as long as she lived, your kindness to her would never be forgotten. ' Poor old Margot's joy was excessive at this intelligence; she clasped her hands, and uttered an exclamation of thankfulness for the good news which Michel had brought. It seemed as if a weight had been lifted off her heart; and after a while she confessed that, notwithstanding the assurances of her relatives that they had no hand in the disappearance of the little girl, she could not divest herself of the idea, that they had somehow made away with her either at the instigation of the priest, or for some reason of their own. 'Now,' she said, 'I feel as happy as I ever can be in this world; for I know that the sin of murder does not rest on my husband or my son. Oh, Monsieur Michel, you do not know how that thought has haunted me. It has brought me to the brink of the grave; it has been with me day and night; and although it is not long since all this happened, it has seemed years to me. '

Jacques, fearing an interruption from either Mathurin Simon or his father, told the poor woman, in a few words, how Monsieur de l'Orme had discovered his daughter, and the way he had managed to deliver her from bondage. He then rose to take leave. Margot thanked him for his kindness, and said, 'God has been very good to me, much more so than I deserve. Should you ever see that dear child again, will you tell her, that the example of her patience and humility has, I trust, made a different woman of me. I know I shall never see her again on earth, but I trust to meet her in heaven. '

Marguerite Simon did not live many months after the miller's visit. Her constitution had received a shock from which she never perfectly rallied, and she declined day by day. As life wanted, she became more and more gentle in her manner, and even her unkind relatives had no excuse for abusing or ill-treating her. As time went by, she became more feeble, and seldom crossed the threshold; when she did so, it was to get something necessary for her household work, which her husband or son had churlishly refused to bring in for her; and it was often with great difficulty that she could manage to fill her pitcher at the well, or bring in the vegetables required for the daily consumption of the family. The domestic animals, too, she had not strength to look after, except at intervals; and when she was utterly incapable of attending to them, she enlisted old Marcel as her assistant. With her declining strength, and her many troubles, Marguerite Simon found great peace at the last; the remembrance of her little companion's sweet face was constantly present to her ; and she beguiled the solitary hours, by trying to recollect the words she had heard her speak, and the hymns she used to sing. Truly, the good seed had been sown, and was bringing forth fruit in the hitherto parched soil of Margot's heart.

The end came at last; and Simon and his son were called upon to resign what they had never prized whilst it was theirs. For a brief space they felt sorry for the past, when the wife and mother they had so neglected and ill-used, passed away from their power; and in answer to her earnest supplication, they promised to try to amend their lives. The bed of death had for a short time a solemnizing effect on them; but it was not of long duration; they soon relapsed into their former habits, and lived and died avoided by all good men.

Jacques Michel never did see Suzanne de l'Orme again, or any member of her family; he shortly afterwards made his escape, and found refuge in Holland. The Prince of Orange, afterwards

William III, of England, offered and afforded protection to such of the Huguenots as chose to make his country their home. The hatred of the Prince for Louis XIV. , on account of the arbitrary measures he adopted with regard to his Protestant subjects – a feeling which was shared by many of the other European powers – was only equalled by his indignation at that monarch's insatiable ambition, which he was determined to check by every means in his power. He therefore afforded every facility to the unhappy persons who had incurred the enmity of the French government, and numbers availed themselves of it, to fly from France, and place themselves under the protection of a Prince, who was not only willing, but able to help them in their time of need.

After Michel had been settled in Holland, he found an opportunity of sending to Suzanne Margot's message to the child who had been her companion for so many weary months; and also having obtained information as to the fate of Monsieur Morin he was at the same time enabled to transmit it to the friends who loved him so well.

THE GOOD PASTOR

S hortly after the miller's return to Saumur, he heard, from an eye-witness an account of the good pastor's sad fate. It will be remembered that Monsieur Morin had been sent on a mission to a distant part of France. The object of this mission was to co-operate with some of his fellow-workers in their endeavours to soothe and pacify the spirit of animosity, which pervaded the two different parties then dividing the Church of Christ in France. It was no easy task to do so; for the pastors of the Reformed faith having been forbidden to assemble their flock for religious worship, it was next to impossible for them to intercede openly with the opposite party for those of their own members who had met in direct contravention of the law. They would only have endangered their lives uselessly, and without benefit to those implicated. It was only possible, therefore, for the more moderate of the pastors, to visit secretly the districts where the Protestants were settled, and exhort and encourage them to prudence in the expression of their sentiments, until better times should dawn on their own peculiar branch of the church.

There were some of their colleagues who did not hold such moderate opinions; and who thought they were doing God acceptable service, by inciting their congregations to assemble, in defiance of the law then in force. They did not reflect that hundreds of innocent persons, children especially, were sacrificed to their extreme views, who might have lived in peace and safety, and perhaps, in a short time, have been allowed to worship God in their own way, if the opposite party had not been exasperated against them.

It must not be supposed that all Huguenots were good men. Some there were, who had embraced the doctrine of the Protestants from expediency, or the love of change. When troubles came they were as anxious to leave that community, and return to the bosom of the Romish Church, as they had been to quit it. These became spies on their unsuspecting brethren, and often gave information which led to their capture and imprisonment. Others, whose zeal outran their discretion, courted persecution, and even martyrdom, in order to show the world what they could endure, and provoked their enemies to perform deeds of greater cruelty, than perhaps they would have committed. These men paraded their opinions on all occasions, never thinking that by doing so, they were making those less enlightened than themselves to sin more deeply than they would otherwise have done. But many – and by far the greater number – were impressed with that Christian charity 'which hopeth all things, and endureth all things,' and were content , in humility and meekness, to await God's pleasure in effecting the re-establishment of the faith in their native land.

Among these last was Monsieur Morin. His piety was genuine, and his love for the Reformed faith an abiding principle. As long as he could by his exertions save any member of his flock from persecution, or make himself useful to them, he did so cheerfully, regardless of the consequences to himself. As we have seen before, nothing could induce him to abandon his post. His courage in danger was just as great as that of some, who rushed blindly to the fate which certainly awaited those who made themselves obnoxious to the existing government; and he showed in the end, that he feared not to lay down his life for the Master whose minister he was.

He, along with two other pastors of equal moderation as himself, was sent to Toulouse, or rather to a village in the environs of that city, where certain fanatical members of the Reformed faith had been compromising the cause by their intemperate demonstrations; and these good men were enjoined to call upon all true-hearted Protestants to remain faithful to their king, as long as it was possible to do so, and to abstain from any violent acts against their enemies.

True, they had ample cause for dissatisfaction; and the cruel indignities to which some of the Protestant families had been exposed, excited the minds of even the most sober-minded and temperate among them. They could not, however, get redress, or better themselves in any way, by their own endeavours; and it was sheer madness to provoke the fury of their bigoted and implacable antagonists. Monsieur Morin and his colleagues were instructed to go down amongst the members of that turbulent faction, and try if their authority and example would be of any use in allaying the storm of angry passions which was then raging. They therefore set out, but with great caution. For a considerable part of the way they were obliged to travel separately, for fear of exciting suspicion; and Monsieur Morin arrived at the appointed place before the two others, some circumstance having occurred to retard one of them; whilst the other had been forced to go by a longer road, to avoid a party of dragoons, who were scouring the country in search of some unhappy wretches, who had been denounced as heretics.

Great was Monsieur Morin's surprise and sorrow, on his

arrival at his place of destination, to find that the public mind was in a state of almost uncontrollable excitement; and he endeavoured to soothe and pacify his vexed and indignant brethren, to the utmost of his power. It was, however, no easy task, although there were not many left to persuade as the sequel will show.

Monsieur Morin, among other things, learnt that meetings had been held in various retired spots; some without being discovered; which had emboldened those who organised them, to hold others in the same way, once they were debarred from attending their usual places of worship. An assemblage of some twenty or thirty people had accordingly met the previous evening, and had been addressed – not by one of their pastors, but by a layman, a landed proprietor of the neighbourhood who was a very zealous and rash upholder of the Reformed principles.

The place of meeting was on the banks of a small river, about a mile from the hamlet which Monsieur Morin had been directed to make his resting-place. A large exhausted quarry, receding considerably from the stream, form a sort of amphitheatre, which made a convenient place for an assemblage of the kind. Trees grew on the top of this quarry, and cast their long fantastic shadows over the open space beneath, and on the quiet and decorous groups reposing there; and creeping plants hung in luxuriant festoons from every fissure and crevice in the embankment, leaving exposed every here and there fragments of stone covered with lichens of various hues.

It was a picturesque and soul-stirring sight, to see those staunch-hearted Reformers, regardless of every danger, resting after their day's toil was over, and listening attentively to the words, which he who addressed them poured forth with a sort of rugged eloquence calculated to attract the sympathies of his listeners. Old men were there – men whose span of life was nearly done – whose whole existence had been one of toil and anxiety, but who had maintained in the midst of the turmoil and vexations of the age, their allegiance to their creed in all simplicity and honesty; and who were willing to lay down what remained of life in its defence. Maidens were there – in the bloom of youth and beauty – endangering their lives, so as to enjoy the privilege or worshipping God, as they had been taught in their infancy; and counting danger as nothing in comparison with duty to their Maker. They reckoned not that he, who had invited them to meet in that sequestered spot, had no right to do so: they only felt that they were doing their duty in assembling for worship, under any circumstances; and in the absence of their legitimate ministers, they accepted him as their representative. Strong men, too, were there – whose bronzed faces told truly that they were sons of that southern clime; and even children had accompanied their parents tot this gathering, fraught with danger though it was. Mistaken these poor people might be, but there was a sublimity in their courageous exposure of themselves to peril, which commanded the respect of all right-minded people.

Yes! It was a pleasant sight. The Reformers, as they arrived at the spot, sat or stood in groups, awaiting the arrival of Monsieur de la Ferriére, the gentleman who had volunteered to address them. The quaintness of the costume of that period, added to the picturesque features of the scene; and a painter would have rejoiced at the opportunity of transmitting it to posterity. The women – some with caps of snowy whiteness, others with bright coloured kerchiefs bound round their heads, and fastened coquettishly on one side – their short petticoats displayed neatly turned ankles, and shoes with antique silver buckles, or wooden sabots, according to the means of the wearer. The younger men, with their dark cloth garments, relieved by scarlet or bright blue scarves wound round their waists, and contrasting with the whiteness of their shirts, which, though coarse in texture, had been bleached in the almost tropical heat of the sun – their woollen caps or 'berets,' as they are called, borrowed from their Pyrean or Basque brethren, added to the quaintness of their costume; and took away from the sombreness of the hues adopted by the older members of the party. The inhabitants of the

143

country districts had not followed the example of their brethren living in cities, in the adoption of sad-coloured textures for their clothing – they all, with few exceptions, adhered to the customs of their ancestors, and wore, with scarcely any difference in make or manufacture, articles of clothing such as were worn a century before.

These good people whiled away the time in discoursing on the topics then uppermost in the minds of all, gentle or simple; and after a short space Monsieur de la Ferriére, at whose invitation they had assembled, having arrived, they began their religious exercises. They commenced with prayers and hymns. Very solemn was the sound of those earnest voices ascending up to heaven, in the calm stillness of the eventide, and sincere and ardent were the petitions which arose in the hearts of most of the worshippers there. They felt the need of help, in the present evil times; and who could give that help, but He who overrules all things, and who brings forth good out of what is seemingly the reverse, to the finite understandings of men? Doubtless, the prayers of these single-minded people went up to the throne of grace, and were acceptable to the Lord who is control of all things.

This part of the proceedings having come to an end, the leader of the little band addressed his hearers on the subject of their grievances. All was so still that his voice rang out with extraordinary distinctness; and as he was fearless in his manner of denouncing the oppressors of the people, and regardless of the consequences thereby incurred, the words he used were more forcible than complimentary to those then in power. He little knew that his circle of auditors was considerably larger than what he actually saw; that enemies, as well as friends were listeners to his intemperate address – enemies who, though unseen, were all the more dangerous, and who were ready to pounce upon him and his unfortunate hearers, at the behest of their leader.

A former member of the community, who had consulted his safety and comfort by turning informer, and by abjuring his faith at the expense of his conscience and of his honour, betrayed his unsuspecting brethren into the hands of a party of soldiers who had been sent in quest of them. The dragoons came upon the little party suddenly – being surely guided to the retired spot which they had chosen for their 'rendezvous,' by the recreant Huguenot, who had sold them to their enemies – and there was no time for flight.

But even had he been aware of the hidden danger, Monsieur de la Ferriére would have said the very same things, which he then uttered in ignorance of the vicinity of the foes of his creed. He thought it his duty to oppose the tyranny of the reigning powers to the utmost of his ability, and no motive of personal safety could deter him from expressing his opinions, at all times whether seasonable or not. In his harangue he inveighed against the king for his intolerance; against his ministers, for encouraging him in his cruel persecution of the Reformers; and against the members of the Romish faith generally, for aiding and abetting their oppressors, in capturing and otherwise molesting their Protestant brethren; and wound up by calling upon all true-hearted Calvinists to make a firm stand against the tyrannous measures then being enacted. The concealed enemies of the Reformed faith, therefore, heard sentiments expressed, which not only exasperated them, but which roused their evil passions to a pitch of uncontrollable frenzy. The command being given, the soldiers rushed upon the betrayed party, and being overpowered, and compelled to surrender, they were carried to Toulouse, and thrown into prison; there to await their trial and their doom. One or two of the most agile managed to escape in the confusion, but all the others fell victims to treachery and fanaticism.

Sad was Monsieur Morin to hear such evil tidings; but the deed was done, and there was no help for it now. He must at every risk see and console his unhappy brethren in this sore strait, and try all in his power to mitigate their sufferings. Let it not be supposed that he, or any other Huguenot holding the same temperate views, refrained from expressing their sentiments at any time that there was a necessity for doing so; on the contrary, they were ready to avow and uphold their creed when called upon to do so, and even seal with their blood their allegiance to their God; but what they deplored and deprecated, was the useless sacrifice of life which was sure to follow rash demonstrations, such as the one which had just occurred. The time was not so far distant, when the Roman Catholic and the Protestant subjects of the kings of France had been arrayed against each other in deadly strife – brother fighting against brother, in the ranks of contending armies. The horrors of civil war could be remembered by some amongst them, and the right-minded on both sides dreaded a renewal of those scenes of bloodshed which had devastated the land – scenes which, if not within their actual recollection, had been handed down by those who had taken part either on one side or the other. True, the Huguenots had often been victorious; but that was, when they had leaders capable of commanding them – men of experience in warfare, and who were as brave as they were experienced. Forces, too, they had, of sufficient strength to cope with their enemies; but now they possessed neither of these advantages, and it would have been wiser to wait in patience, until it would please God to soften the hearts of their foes, instead of rushing headlong to destruction.

Monsieur Morin explained all this to those who were left to listen to his exhortations. He showed them the folly of having met at the suggestion of one, who, however sincere he might be in his attachment to the Reformed faith, had no authority to convene any meeting of the sort, and that they had run the risk, and incurred the penalty, of such an act, without gaining any benefit to a single member of the Protestant community. On the contrary, they had only made matters worse by this ill-timed demonstration.

Amongst other details which the good man heard of the proceedings of the previous evening, he learnt that a poor woman had been grievously wounded by one of the soldiers, and had been left on the ground, apparently dead; whilst a young child of hers, who had accompanied his mother to the meeting, had been carried away by the assailants, no one knew whither. The woman had been taken to her home some hours afterwards, having been found and recognized by some neighbours, who were returning from their labour in the fields.

Monsieur Morin inquired where the unfortunate woman lived, and signified his intention of going to see if he could render any assistance in this distressing case. The farmer and his wife, at whose house he had stopped, insisted on his taking some refreshment before proceeding thither, after which, the former offered to guide him to the cottage of the sufferer. Weary and sad, the good pastor then went with his companion on his charitable errand.

Murder

When the Huguenot pastor and his guide arrived at the farm house, where the ministry of the former was so much needed, they heard subdued sounds of sorrow, and on entering found they had just come in time to see the woman die. She was lying on a couch, which had been hastily prepared in one of the lower rooms of the house, when she was brought home by her terrified and sympathizing neighbours. Her husband was standing near her, and she was speaking to him words of consolation in low, broken accents, as Monsieur Morin and his companion entered. At a glance he saw that her end was near, and at once approaching, he knelt down and offered up heartfelt prayers for her departing soul. A look of perfect peace rested on her pallid countenance, as she faintly responded to the solemn words uttered by the holy man, who was endangering his life in ministering to her comfort. Her husband stood stern and rigid, gazing gloomily on his dying wife, and scarcely seeming to understand the words which fell from the lips of Monsieur Morin, so absorbed was he in contemplating the wreck before him. He seemed stunned by the suddenness of the calamity which had fallen on him, and could not yet believe in its reality, or accept the cross which was laid on him. A heavy cross it was! A few hours before the outrage which deprived him of his wife, the unhappy man had parted from her, apparently secure of a long life of happiness with her. She was young, and full of health and spirits, and attached to her husband by bonds of affection, pure and genuine; and affection which was returned by him in kind. They had an only child, the joy of their hearts, on whom they built fond hopes for the future. What was that future now? A blank: his wife murdered – his child torn from him – oh! It was a heavy cross indeed! Alas! He had yet to learn that sorrows are sent in mercy, and are but blessings in disguise.

The prayer at last was ended, and all around waited in silence for the end of one, who, but the day before, had been so full of health and vigour. Fainter and fainter became the breathing of the poor woman, and still she turned her dying eyes towards her husband, who, in his turn, never took his face off her. It seemed as if she wished to implore him to forgive the authors of all this misery, but the power of speech was gone; and the wretched man was at moment too overcome with grief, to listen to the suggestions of his better nature; or, to notice or heed the mute appeal of his wife.

They had been standing thus for some minutes, when the trampling of horses was heard without; immediately followed by a loud rap at the door, which, opening at the same time, admitted a tall, commanding-looking man, wearing a military uniform. He was followed by several armed men, who entered the room, and ranged themselves behind him. Monsieur Morin raised his hand, and silently pointing to the couch, near to which he stood, by a gesture implored a few moments' forbearance. The officer, for such was his rank, instantly raised his plumed hat from his head, and signing to his men to leave the room, remained profoundly silent, a not unmoved spectator of the scene before him. He had not long to wait- in a few short moments the departing spirit had left its earthly tenement, and returned to the God who gave it. The widowed, childless man struggled hard to maintain his composure; but it was useless – his young wife lay dead, killed by the ruthless cruelty of those whom she had never harmed; and his only child had been carried away, he knew not whither. What wonder, then, that the whole world seemed a blank to him, and that regardless of the presence of friends or foes, he threw himself on his knees, and groaned aloud in the anguish of his spirit.

The Huguenot Pastor offered up a prayer for consolation to come to the bereaved man, who was crushed to the earth by the magnitude of the sorrow which had so suddenly fallen upon him; and at the same time implored pardon for the wretched perpetrators of the cruel deed. His eloquence, and the simple dignity of his manner, struck wonder into the heart of one of his listeners. Kindly disposed as he was towards the persecuted members of the Reformed church, that listener had never had occasion to meet any of her appointed ministers, except in a casual manner. His knowledge of the Protestants, and their peculiar tenets, was therefore limited, and he had never before heard words like those, so forcibly conveyed by the venerable man at that solemn moment; and as those earnest tones fell upon his ear, he resolved, that, whatever might be the consequence, he never more would be instrumental in seeking out and capturing any member of the Reformed persuasion. He was obliged to perform the duty on which he had been sent that day; but that duty once done, he would find means of leaving the country, and a service which had no longer any attractions for an honourable and conscientious man.

As soon as his prayer was ended, Monsieur Morin advanced calmly to the officer, and requested to know the purport of his visit. This was soon said, and the young man told the aged minister, in words of profound respect and sorrow, that his object in being there was to apprehend him, and take him back to Toulouse; for, he added, 'I am not mistaken in supposing you are Monsieur Louis Morin?'

'No, sir! My name is Louis Morin; I would accompany you instantly, but I have a duty to perform, which, I trust, you will not prevent. You see that poor dead woman; she cannot be left thus, and who is there to bury her but me? Will you therefore permit me to stay until her body has been carried to its last resting-place? I pledge myself solemnly, then, not to attempt to escape, but to follow you wherever it may be your pleasure to take me.'

The officer looked down on a sheet of paper which he held in his hand, as if referring to what was written thereon; but in reality, it was to conceal the emotion he could not repress at the sight of that venerable man, who was so undauntedly fulfilling the task appointed for him; knowing while he did so, that it would bring down heavier punishment on himself. He was lost in admiration, and asked himself the question which others had asked themselves before, 'what there was amiss in a religion which could boast of such men as the one before him?' As soon as he had mastered the feeling, which had for an instant overpowered him, he replied courteously, and granted Monsieur Morin's request, at the same time expressing his regret that he would be obliged to leave one of his men as a guard, as it was against orders to leave a prisoner unwatched; and he hoped Monsieur Morin would forgive his seeming want of faith in him. The good old man told him he perfectly understood his reason for acting thus, and assured him that he did not resent it in the least. The officer then proceeded with the remainder of his duty.

'Jean Ferrand,' he said, addressing the husband of the murdered woman, 'were you at the meeting held last night?'

The man thus addressed rose from his knees, and in a voice of unutterable anguish, exclaimed, 'No, I was not! Would that I had been; this,' pointing to his dead wife, might have been avoided, and I would have been there assuredly. . .'

'Silence!' interrupted his questioner, with feigned displeasure;'reply only to what I ask you, and without comment. Were you at that meeting last night?'

'No, sir!'

'Very well, you are free. And you Jacques Macé, and you Jeannette le Roux, and you Pierre Hubert?'

An answer in the negative being given by each of the individuals addressed, they received the same assurance as Jean Ferrand; and the officer took a kindly leave of the sorrowful inmates; saying, that he would give directions to a man whom he could trust, to remain until Monsieur Morin was ready to accompany him; and he himself would proceed to another village farther on. At the same time, he begged the good pastor to use despatch in performing the sad task he had undertaken, adding 'I wish I could dissuade you from it, for it will only add to the animosity of your enemies ; and aggravate the punishment which will be awarded to you, for belonging to a sect which it has been determined to extirpate. 'Monsieur Morin shook his head, and the officer continued, 'I feel sure that all argument is useless on this point with a man of your stamp; I shall therefore make my request on other grounds, and ask it as a personal favour; for it is at imminent risk to myself that I allow you to stay for such a purpose. '

With another courteous salutation he left the house, having received Monsieur Morin's assurance that there should be as little delay as possible. As soon as he was gone, Jacques Macé (the man who guided the aged minister to the house), aided by Hubert (Jean Gerrand's farm-servant), constructed a rude bier; whilst Jeannette prepared the body of her mistress for burial. Many were the tears the poor girl shed, whilst fulfilling her sad task; but, they were not altogether tears of sadness. They fell, as much in thankfulness that the unfortunate victim of religious fanaticism was safe from further cruelty, and at her own miraculous escape from imprisonment. While thus occupied, time went on, and at length all was ready.

There was no time for the usual observances on such occasions. All was done in haste, and only a few hours elapsed between the death of Louise Ferrand and her burial.

Shortly before sunset, the murdered woman was carried to the cemetery by her husband and his companions – the soldier walking behind. The good pastor read the service for the dead – it did not take long to do so – and soon she was laid in the narrow resting-place grudgingly allowed to Protestants in the village churchyard. It was one of those calm serene evenings, which seem to bring peace, even to hearts torn with anguish. The sun had slowly sunk in the west, and the grey shadows of twilight were gradually deepening, and casting indistinctness on the surrounding landscape, as the little band of mourners knelt round the new-made grave. Mute prayers for comfort in the deep affliction which had befallen them, but especially for the bereaved husband, arose from the heart of each individual present; and supplications for help in coming troubles, and resignation to whatever it might please the Almighty to send them, were offered up in simple earnestness. As they rose from their knees, a nightingale, concealed in a hawthorn bush close by, poured forth such a gush of thrilling melody, that each stopped to listen with rapt attention. In that solemn hour, it seemed like the song of a seraph, bringing them the assurance that their prayers had been heard and accepted; and that what they had asked in all humility, would be granted by the all-wise Being to whom those prayers had been addressed. All being now over, Monsieur Morin turned to the soldier, who had approached nearer; and said, 'My friend, I am now ready to accompany you. '

'Monsieur' replied Jacques Moulin (for it was our old friend whose privilege it was to guard the Huguenot), 'you must go back to the house, to take rest and refreshment before proceeding further. Monsieur d'Aureville's commands were that we should remain until his return, which cannot be yet for some hours. '

'Monsieur d'Aureville!' exclaimed the pastor, 'is that

gentleman Monsieur d'Aureville?'

'Yes, without doubt! Did you not know it?'

'No, my friend. But I might have guessed it, from the kindness and consideration he has shown this day. Few bear so high a character as he does, and not undeservedly, as I can testify from experience. I had often heard of his courtesy and kind feeling for our unhappy people; but, I never had the opportunity of meeting him. God will reward him for his forbearance and Christian charity.'

Discoursing thus, they reached Ferrand's house. The old man gladly availed himself of the chance of taking that rest which his bodily and mental exertions had rendered necessary, and in spite of the danger which menaced him, he slept calmly for some hours. The period of Monsieur d'Aureville's absence was somewhat lengthened; but, when he returned, Monsieur Morin was ready, when summoned to accompany him. He was provided with a horse, as the distance to Toulouse from thence was too great for a man of his years to accomplish on foot – and thus they journeyed on, and in due time arrived at their destination.

SAFE AT LAST

After the funeral of his wife, Jean Ferrand returned to his cottage sad at heart and weary. He felt crushed to the earth by the suddenness of his misfortune, and did not seem to care what became of him. As night came on, the feeling of utter desolation became more intensified; and he could find neither repose nor consolation in any thing. His thoughts constantly reverted to the past – the image of his wife and child haunted him perpetually, and he became a prey to the most fearful anguish. He tossed about on his couch, and tried to sleep; but it was useless – the feverish restlessness which had taken hold of him, was too great for repose. His mind also was torn by conflicting emotions, he could not bring himself to forgive the authors of his misery; and he wearied himself with forming schemes of vengeance, against those who had worked such evil for him.

Jean Ferrand was a good man in the main, and had he been left in peaceful possession of his home, and allowed to worship God according to the dictates of his conscience, no doubt he would have remained loyal to his king and country; but the wicked persecution to which himself and his co-religionists were subjected, had unsettled his mind, and this last act of wanton cruelty excited his wrath to such a pitch, that he forgot the pleading of his dying wife for their enemies, in his desire to revenge her death and his wrongs.

He turned many plans in his mind – wild plans they were – plans which, if carried in to effect, would have brought certain and rapid destruction on himself; but he thought not of that in his desolation – besides, what was life to him, bereft of all which had made it dear? If his child – his little Henri, had only been left to him, he would still have had some one to live for; and he would have battled with his grief for the sake of the helpless being dependant on him; but for aught he knew to the contrary, the child had been as ruthlessly butchered as his mother – no trace had been seen of him since the conflict, and even if he still lived, there was no hope of his ever being found again. He was probably at that moment immured in some convent, well and kindly treated perhaps, by reason of his tender age; but, for ever separated from his broken-hearted father. The child was only two years old, and did not even know his name; and, after the strangeness and terror of being thrown entirely among strangers had passed away, would soon become reconciled to his new home, and become quite happy in it.

The hours pass slowly by, and at length faint streaks of light in the east announced the approach of another day. Monsieur Morin and his escort had taken their departure before the dawn, and the cottage of Jean Ferrand was left in perfect quiet; all slept save the wretched owner; and overpowered by the feeling of vengeful animosity which had entered his heart and gained the mastery there, he arose with the determination to go forth as the avenger of blood. Waiting until his two servants were astir, and gloomily telling them he was going away, and might be absent sometime, he bade them take care of the house, until his return. He then turned his steps towards Toulouse, leaving to chance his subsequent movement.

After walking about two miles Ferrand came to a small hamlet; here the craving of hunger assailed him, for he had tasted no food since his wife's death. He thought he would enter one of the scattered cottages of which the hamlet was composed, and ask the hospitality of the inmates: for he knew them a little from their neighbourhood to his own dwelling, and he did not doubt their willingness to give him a morsel of bread. Poor man! He much needed repose and refreshment – his lips were parched from the inward fever which consumed him, and his eyes had a restless glare in them, indicating the storm of angry feeling which agitated his mind. Usually a healthy fine-complexioned man, whose sunburnt features were pleasant to behold – Jean Ferrand had become almost unrecognisable. There was a haggard, pinched look about his face, which told plainly of the fierce conflict raging within; his dress, heretofore neat though homely, was now disordered and neglected, and he looked as if ten years had been added to his life, during the short space which had elapsed since his earthly happiness had been destroyed.

Ferrand seemed lost to all that was going on around him; but exhausted, nature at length asserted her rights, and the wretched man felt that he must have rest and sustenance, before he could proceed on the mission he had marked out for himself. He sat down for a few moments on a stone bench outside the cottage he proposed entering, feeling too much exhausted even to ask for admission; when suddenly the door opened, and out ran a little boy, followed by a girl two or three years older. Jean Ferrand turned to see who had come out, and his gaze rested on his own little Henri, - his only child! Was it a dream, or was it a reality? Ah! He was not left long in doubt, the little one recognised his father, and ran into his out-stretched arms, as into a sure refuge. The little fair head nestled against the strong man's breast, and the childish voice asked, in lisping loving accents for his poor mother.

The heart of the father was rent with agony at the touching question, and had not a burst of tears relieved him, he must have fallen senseless to the ground. Happily, tears did come; at first like a fierce tempest, threatening to overwhelm the stricken man, and then gradually falling more softly; like the gentle showers of spring, which softening the earth, make it ready to receive the seed which the labourer sows; so Jean Ferrand's heart, which had become hardened and withered by the whirlwind of persecution, became, through the instrumentality of a child, soft and yielding, and ready to forego his schemes of revenge for that little child's sake.

When he became calm, his first thought was one of curiosity, as to how little Henri had come to that spot; but he vainly inquired of him; he only murmured some unconnected words about soldiers and horses, but nothing which his father could understand. The little girl, who had come out of the cottage with Henri, had meanwhile gone in to call her mother; and the good woman now stood on the threshold waiting till the storm of grief, which overpowered Jean Ferrand, should have spent itself, to come near and explain all she knew about his son. She now told him, that on the evening the murder of his wife took place, as she was occupied in preparing her husband's supper, she heard a great noise; and amidst the trampling of horses' feet and the clanking of sabres, she could hear the shouts of men, and the screams of women and children. She ran to the door to see what the tumult meant, and at that moment the party of dragoons who had murdered poor Louise Ferrand passed with their captives. One of the dragoons had a little child seated in front of him who was crying with terror at the sight and sounds around him. Just as the party passed the house, one of the Huguenots managed to slip away from his captor, and the fear of being re-taken lending wings to his feet, he fled with extraordinary rapidity along the road they had just travelled. The suddenness of the action, for a moment, took the soldiers by surprise, and thus gave the fugitive a chance of escape. In a very short space of time, however, they recovered from their astonishment, and two or three set off in hot pursuit; amongst them, the man who had little Henri in front of him. He probably thought that so young a child would impede his progress, and with an oath, he flung him on the ground not far from the place where the woman stood, quite regardless of the poor child's cries of pain and terror. The good woman, with a mother's instinct, rushed forward and caught hold of the helpless little one, and vanished indoors before any one had time to notice the circumstance; and the rest of the dragoons, encumbered as they were with prisoners, proceeded on their way to Toulouse, without perceiving that any of the party was missing, and leaving their comrades to follow as they could. She concluded her tale by saying, that she hoped the poor fugitive had escaped; for the dragoons had passed again some hours later, and although it was nearly dark, she felt sure she must have seen if they had any prisoner with them; and they were riding slowly, as if dispirited by want of success. But, 'Monsieur Ferrand,' she added, 'come in and have something to eat, you look faint and tired, and a good breakfast will restore you. '

'Are you not afraid of succouring a Huguenot in his distress, Madame Bertrand?'

'Oh! No,' she replied, 'my husband and I are good Catholics, but we are not advocates for persecution: nevertheless, when you have rested sufficiently, I shall not press you to stay – you know I must be cautious for the sake of my children:' then turning to a girl, older than the little one who had run out of the cottage with Henri Ferrand, she said, 'Annette, mon enfant, help me to get breakfast ready at once. '

The homely but plentiful repast was soon on the table; and her husband having meanwhile come in, Madame Bertrand invited her guest to take a seat, and pressed him to partake of the food which was placed before him. The prattle of little Henri, and the hospitality of his kind-hearted entertainers, beguiled the grief-stricken man into momentary forgetfulness of his sorrows; and for a brief space he was happier than he had fancied he could be again in this world.

The meal ended, he got up to take leave of his friends, and tried to thank them for their kindness to himself and his child – but the effort was too great – the image of his lost Louise rose before him, and choked his utterance; he could only wring their hands in token of farewell; and snatching up the little boy, he left the cottage amidst the tears and sobs of its inmates, who invoked blessings on his head, and on that of the child, who had been so miraculously restored to him.

Slowly and sadly he retraced his steps towards his desolate home – a home once so happy! It was still early in the day, and when he lifted the latch, the sun streamed in at the open door, making the darkened room for an instant look almost cheerful. Alas! The absence of the being who had been the life and happiness of that dwelling, was not more keenly felt than at the actual time of her death; then the shock was so great, as almost to paralyse thought, and benumb the faculties of her unhappy husband: now – the full extent of his misery, and the loneliness of his future life, seemed spread out before him, and Jean Ferrand felt that he was indeed and in truth, alone in the world. The gleam of sunshine which had come in at the open door, was shut out again, and the gloom deeper than it was before. Lost in thought, Ferrand pondered over his hard lot; and he was nearly giving way to despair again, when the artless prattle of the little boy once more roused him to a sense of his duty, and his better angel whispered to him words of hope and consolation. After a brief mental prayer for strength and resignation, he took his child in his arms, and kneeling down, he vowed he would bring up that child in the fear of the Lord, and dedicated himself and his son to the service of Him who gave, and had taken away the great blessing of his life. He arose strengthened to do battle with his foes, but not in the sense which in his mad wrath he had contemplated some hours before. His vengeful feelings gave way to softer emotions, and although he felt his wrongs as keenly, he left it to his God to avenge them. Little Henri, young as he was, saw that his father was much disturbed; he crept away to a corner of the room, wondering at the unusual stillness which reigned around, but in his childish simplicity never even thinking of asking what it meant.

After some reflection, Jean Ferrand summoned his servants. They were both occupied in their usual duties about the farm-yard; but when Jeannette heard her master's voice, she ran in, overjoyed at his speedy return; his manner when he left them having given both to herself and Pierre, the impression that he meditated a long journey. When she saw the child, her joy was increased ten fold; and she devoured him with caresses, which he returned with interest, whilst she eagerly questioned his father as to where he had found him. He replied briefly, and desired her to call Pierre, who did not appear to have heard his summons. When the latter entered the room, Ferrand proceeded to tell them that he had come to the determination of leaving France forthwith, and of seeking a home in some more tolerant and peaceful country. They were scarcely surprised at this announcement, for truth to tell, it was a subject which occupied most men's minds at that period; and many were the secret preparations made for flying from a land where life and property were so constantly in peril. Pierre Hubert and his fellow-servant had few worldly goods to dispose of; but they had laid by their savings, and spent as little of their wages as possible, so as to have the means at command for leaving their unhappy country whenever there should be any need for doing so.

Jean Ferrand, though not a wealthy man, had enough to live on comfortably; and from time to time had disposed of portions of his property, in a quiet way, as thousands of his fellow-subjects had done, and were doing, foreseeing the necessity there would soon be for immediate flight. He had accordingly amassed a considerable sum, and having with the assistance of Jeannette, who was a distant relative concealed it about his person; he next proceeded to put together such of his little valuables as he could carry. Pierre and Jeannette, who were both much attached to their master, and who equally belonged to the Reformed Church, begged earnestly to be allowed to accompany him; but he told them he could not longer afford to give them wages, and must in future live very frugally – perhaps hardly, so as to have the means of bringing up his son; but he highly approved of their determination to leave France, and hoped, if they succeeded in making their escape, that it would please God to enable them to meet again. He told them it was his intention, if possible, to cross the frontier into Switzerland; a difficult undertaking, and fraught with great danger, and he feared being captured in the attempt; more perhaps for his little Henri's sake than for himself. As far as he was concerned, their bitter persecutors could only kill his body, they could not take away his belief, and God would sustain him through whatever pain and torment they might inflict; but it would be far different with his child; if he survived he would most assuredly be brought up in the Roman Catholic faith – a faith which he knew to be so full or error, that it was agony to his mind, even to think of such a possibility. Far, far better would it be to lay the innocent little one in his grave, hard though the task would be to the loving parent. To avoid such a calamity as capture or discovery the greatest caution must be used, and he must try to cross the boundary between the two countries unobserved.

Jean Ferrand would much have liked the companionship of his two faithful servants; they had lived with him many years, and were more like old friends than servants. They were under promise of marriage, when they should each have amassed a sufficient sum of money to begin housekeeping, and their master and mistress had long been aware of this agreement and had given their hearty concurrence to it. What wonder then, that after a few more endeavours to permit them to be the companions of his flight, Jean Ferrand yielded, and the plan of expatriation was canvassed and finally agreed to; more especially as little Henri was so young, that a woman's care was almost an absolute necessity. Jeannette le Roux took care to make that circumstance her principal 'point d'appui,' and said she wanted no wages; it would be a labour of love with her to attend to the little boy she was so fond of: and as for Pierre, he was quite of his good Jeannette's way of thinking, and would work for both in the new country they were going to. And thus it was decided.

Their poor sorrowing master was not the least pleased at the decision, for it had been a great trial to him to go forth alone among strangers; this offer of companionship in his wanderings, therefore, contributed more to soothe his sorrow than anything else could have done. This point settled, they proceeded to discuss plans for the future, amongst which was one that gradually took hold of their minds, and seemed to be the most feasible of any yet discussed. This plan, when developed, presented many obstacles, but still it was the only one which appeared to hold out any hope of success; and these melted away at the energetic suggestions of its proposer, who, in conjunction with Jeannette, was determined to see everything in a bright light, and both were sanguine as to the ultimate advantage to be derived from undertaking it. Pierre Hubert had a cousin who lived near the frontier; he possessed a small farm, and although a good Catholic himself, was known among the Reformers as one, who would scorn to lend himself to any of the deeds of villainy, which were then perpetrated in too many parts of France. He was strict in the observances of his creed, so that no one could cast the shadow of suspicion on him – he obeyed the laws of his country and feared his king, but he feared his God more; and he would no more have taken the life of a fellow-creature, or give information by which that life could be taken or even endangered, on the ground of difference of opinion in religious matters, than he would have forsaken the religion which he believed of all others, to be the best.

DANGER AND DRAGOONS

Through the instrumentality then, of this cousin of Pierre Hubert, it was proposed that their escape from the kingdom should be attempted and Pierre Hubert never for one moment doubted his willingness to assist in the undertaking. Quietly then, they discussed the ways and means of accomplishing their perilous journey. Jean Ferrand would not submit to be separated from his child, and it was running too great a risk for four people to travel together in those times of danger and suspicion – at any rate it would not do to leave the house all at the same moment. It was therefore agreed that Pierre should remain behind, and follow the next night; whilst Jean and his little son, accompanied by Jeannette, should leave that very day as soon as it was sufficiently dark to ensure their exciting no observation. They must walk too, for the lumbering carts of those days were not calculated for travellers who wished to go in secret; but Pierre suggested that they should stop in the neighbourhood of a village a few leagues off, and wait there until he should rejoin them; he might then load his master's cart with hay or straw, as he had often done before, and pretend he was conveying it to some distant place for sale; and he could so contrive, that when they arrived at their halting-place, Jeannette and the little boy might be concealed under the load, and thereby escape observation. Provisions too, could be carried in that way; and they need not therefore be under the necessity of trusting to chance for appeasing their hunger. This last arrangement respecting the cart was hailed with delight; for Jeannette would soon have tired of carrying the child, who was too young to walk any distance, and his father could be of little help to her, burdened as he was, with the little store of valuables and necessaries he had collected to bring away.

Everything being satisfactorily settled, they all busied themselves in making the needful preparations for their journey. Very sorrowfully they at length left the cottage – endeared to them by years of happiness passed under its roof - but there was no help for it. It could no longer afford them shelter, for, at any moment, the infuriated soldiery of a despotic and tyrannical monarch might make another raid on the district; and Jean Ferrand being now a marked man, it might go hard with him, and with his household, should any of them be found in their old home. Monsieur d'Aureville's forbearance and pitying consideration had saved them for the time, from the imminent peril in which they stood, but other leaders would probably succeed him, who would have far less kindly feelings towards the Huguenots than he had, and who would not listen to the dictates of humanity in fulfilling the duties assigned to them. Nay! Many and by far the greater number, revelled in the discomfort of the 'heretics,' as the Reformers were popularly called, and aggravated by every means in their power the torments of the unhappy people who had the misfortune to fall into their hands. Flight was therefore their only resource, and when all was ready they went forth.

Jeannette was enveloped in a large, dark mantle, beneath which she carried the little boy, who was fast asleep, and all unconscious of the grief of those who were risking so much to ensure his safety as well as their own. Pierre Hubert dared not accompany them; but the hope of re-union cheered him in his solitude, and after their departure, he busied himself in getting all ready for his own journey. It was late in the night when he had finished his work; he had just eaten a morsel, and was preparing to take a few hours rest, when a low tap at the door startled him. He listened intently, scarcely daring to breathe, when just as he was beginning to fancy his imagination had deceived him, he again heard the same sound, but a little louder than before, and a voice in subdued accents called out, 'Jean Ferrand, are you there? Let me in, for the love of God!'

Pierre, although he did not recognise the voice, immediately answered and said, 'Who are you? What do you want?'

'I am François Martel! Do not keep me out, I implore you; for I am half dead with fatigue and hunger!'

'François Martel!' exclaimed Pierre, hastily unbarring the door; 'why, man, I thought you safe in the prison at Toulouse!'

'Exactly, and so I would have been, but for these good legs of mine,' rejoined the new comer, a tall handsome youth of some eighteen years of age; 'but Pierre, for the love of heaven give me something to eat, I have tasted nothing since that dreadful night when those fiends of dragoons set upon us, with the exception of a few chestnuts which I happened to have in my pocket; and I feel very faint. ' His looks did not belie his words, for he turned ashy-pale, and would have fallen to the ground but for Pierre's sustaining arm; with his disengaged hand, he reached a drinking cup from the table; there was some wine still left in it, and holding it to the poor fellow's lips, he made him swallow it. This revived him, and in a few moments he had recovered sufficiently to do justice to the food set before him. Pierre Hubert meanwhile trimmed his lamp; and having made sure that the doors were securely barred and bolted, and the shutters

169

made fast, he sat down to learn from his friend the history of the wonderful escape from his captors on that memorable night when poor Louise Ferrand fell victim to their cruelty.

François was young and full of health and energy, and he fled onwards with the speed of a hunted deer, gaining visibly on the men who were so ruthlessly bent on his destruction. Still, the odds were fearful! It was indeed 'a race for life,' and if he failed in eluding his enemies, he knew the penalty would be terrible. On, on, they came, those heavy cavalry horses, thundering along the road; the shouts of the riders and the clanking of their accoutrements rang through his brain, and almost made it reel with agonized dread, notwithstanding his previous confidence in himself. The danger was indeed frightful, great drops stood on his forehead, but still he ran on, ran with such speed, that his feet scarcely seemed to touch the ground. What the result would have been had the poor man been obliged to continue his flight on the high road, it is not difficult to guess; but guided by the hand of Providence, he suddenly darted into a narrow lane on his right, kept straight for a few yards, then bounded over the hedge, and fell on the other side into a deep hole in which grew brambles and rank weeds of every sort. For some moments he lay panting for breath, and pondering in utter bewilderment on the novelty of his position. His hands and face were much scratched and bruised, and his clothes torn in his descent, but otherwise he was not hurt.

Recovering from the surprise caused by his sudden fall, he sat down composedly and philosophically to await the issue, taking the precaution of noiselessly drawing the brambles over his head as an effectual screen from observation. It was now getting dark, a circumstance which certainly was in his favour, as it gave him a better chance of escape, and he inwardly thanked God for having guided him into this hiding place. His feelings can be better imagined than described, when he heard the horses galloping backward and forward along the road, urged on by their baffled riders, who were looking in every direction save the right one, for the person who had so mysteriously disappeared from their sight. The exclamations of the men, and their impotent rage, were rather amusing to François than otherwise, when he was once convinced of the security of his situation. An indomitable spirit seemed to have taken possession of him, and the buoyancy of youth and strength sustained him in the awful peril which he was even then incurring. He was actually but a few yards from his pursuers, but he knew that the lane by which he had come was so narrow, that only one of those ponderous steeds could come on at a time; and he thought the dragoons would scarcely trust themselves singly in such a place, unknown to them, when there was so little light to show them where they were going.

He was right in his conclusions; the men in pursuit of him were new to the work, and had not yet acquired that relish for hunting their fellow-creatures which the older hands in their company had attained. They halted, therefore, and held a parley; so near were they to him, that he could hear them express their dissatisfaction at their want of success, and their belief that it was useless to try to catch the Huguenot; who must be in league with the powers of darkness, to have vanished so suddenly from their view. One of the party suggested firing a few shots down the now dark lane, as a parting remembrance to the fugitive should he happen to be lurking there, and with the hope that one at least of the shots would have effect, and thus point out his place of concealment. Accordingly, each soldier discharged his piece in the direction indicated; and after waiting a few moments to ascertain the result, but hearing nothing, they turned the horses' heads towards their original destination, grumbling audibly at this addition to their already hard day's work. The rescued youth felt the deepest thankfulness for the unspeakable mercy just vouchsafed to him. He had been a Huguenot from his childhood, as his parents were before him, but he had never weighed the merits of his creed against that of the Roman Catholics. Merry and thoughtless, though thoroughly well-meaning and well-principled, he took life easily, and did not stop to consider whether he was serving God in the manner most acceptable to Him. He had been accustomed to that particular mode of worship, and as those with whom his daily lot was cast were Reformers also, he went on doing his duty, to a certain extent, but certainly seldom reflecting as to whether the doctrines of the religion he professed, were in reality the right ones to adopt or not. François took a certain delight in the risks incurred; that, of course, was a feeling which most lads of his age would have shared with him. The fear of being captured by their opponents, was always mingled with a certain enjoyment of the excitement for the Reformers were exposed to continual alarm. It all imparted a tinge of romance to the somewhat monotonous routine which the grave and severe disciples of Calvin usually enforced on their households.

This day, however, had been one of such extreme danger, that it had the effect of sobering, in some degree, the exuberant spirits of the young Huguenot; he felt he had miraculously escaped from the fangs of the blood-thirsty men, who had so nearly re-captured him, and a sense of the imminent peril he had been in, transformed the hitherto thoughtless boy into a thinking man. From that day a shade of seriousness might have been traced in his demeanour; and his bright, happy face assumed an air of gravity, not often perceptible before, and which, without detracting from his former frankness of manner, and joyous expression of countenance, only added sensibility to it; and toned down what might otherwise have been a little too boisterous, but for this restraining power. He had leisure during his unexpected detention, to think over the past, and to make resolutions for the future, and he determined, with God's help, to go on steadfastly resisting temptation to evil; and if need be, to lay down his life rather than turn recreant to his creed.

Slowly the dragoons retraced their steps towards Toulouse, to assist in the sanguinary deeds about to be committed there; and as they passed Bertrand's house, his wife was not wrong in fancying that their chase had been unsuccessful.

Allowing a sufficient time to elapse after their departure, to make sure he would not be observed, the fugitive thought he would emerge from his concealment. There was now no fear of pursuit, for some time at least, and the sooner he could get out of the uncomfortable hole into which he had fallen, the better he would be pleased. It was by no means a pleasant place to be in. It had rained hard some days previously, and there was a tolerable quantity of mud at the bottom of this hole. Noisome insects and creeping things of all sorts began to crawl over him, to his great discomfort; and when he attempted to move, the brambles scratched his hands and face afresh. He was unwilling however to remain where he was, so, carefully pulling aside these unpleasant impediments, he rose to his feet, and tried to feel his way out of his prison. The increasing gloom made it impossible for him to see what sort of a place he had fallen into; but by feeling as high as he could, he found he could not reach the top of the hole, or pit, or whatever it might be in which he was. Had he been able to see, he might perhaps have managed to scramble out; but when he jumped over the hedge, and found himself at the bottom of this unknown abyss, he was too much surprised, and his fear of being discovered was too great, to notice where he was. Whilst the dragoons were there, his whole thoughts were centred on their movements, and by the time they had departed; and he had given them time enough to get clear off; the little light which was left had faded away, and now he was unable to distinguish a spot where he might get a footing, and thus draw himself up to the surface of the earth again. He groped from side to side, as well as he could; but it was not an easy task, and at last he gave up the attempt in despair, concluding that he must wait until it was light, to make his way out. It was a fine night happily – and he resigned himself to his fate with a good grace.

François Martel was of a happy temperament; he was always inclined to look out for a bright side to every dark prospect, and this helped him on wonderfully in through his life. At first he chafed a little at being caught like a mouse in a trap; but he could not help reflecting that, but for that trap, he would in all probability have been shut up in a larger one – the prison at Toulouse; from whence there could be no escape, without passing through much suffering and tribulation. Thankfully then, did he resign himself to the necessity of passing the night where he was; and as there was no possibility of sleeping in the uncomfortable position he was, he whiled away the time in making plans for the future.

François was an orphan with no near relations that he knew of; and moreover, scarcely remembered his parents, being only an infant when they died. All he recollected of his childhood was being taken care of by some neighbours, who took compassion on him when he was left alone. As soon as he was old enough, François was taken into the service of a Huguenot farmer, and with him he had remained until that day of violence, when they were torn from their homes and carried into captivity. He had been fortunate enough to escape; not so his master and mistress; and they were even now undergoing the pains and penalties inflicted on those who professed the Reformed religion. It was of no use to return to the farm, even if he could have done so without danger to himself for the house was desolate; the farmer and his wife having been its sole occupants beside himself. They had children, but they were married and settled in a distant part of France, and were probably themselves fugitives, or imprisoned for their religious opinions. Nothing had been heard of them for a long time; and the chances were, that the little property which belonged to the old people would be confiscated to the Crown. Martel therefore resolved on going as soon as it was practicable, to consult Jean Ferrand, with whom he was acquainted, and on whose judgment he could rely as to his future course in the difficult path which lay before him. Having disposed of this so far to his satisfaction, he now turned his thoughts into another channel, and tried to discover the locality he was in. He could not remember any hole or pit in the neighbourhood of sufficient depth to conceal so completely an individual of his proportions and ransacked his brain for a clue to the mysterious cavity – but in vain, and finally he gave up all speculation on the subject.

At length day dawned, and as the light increased he saw at once where he was. In a corner of the field into which he had leapt, when so closely pursued there had stood a sort of shed or hut, used probably as a shelter for cattle. It had long been disused – so long that the rudely thatched roof had partly fallen in; the walls, which were composed of mud and very thick had resisted the inroads of time, and were still standing; brambles and briars had gradually grown in the hut and over it, so as completely to conceal it from the sight of the passer-by, and tall nettles and long grass rustled side by side with stately ferns and delicate creeping plants. Externally it presented the appearance of an earthen mound, covered abundantly with a luxuriant growth of brushwood and bramble bushes. The field in which it stood was not much frequented, and did not seem to belong to any body in particular; it was a sort of common property, and a favourite place of resort for the little peasant children of the neighbourhood, who often plucked the pleasant tasting berries growing on these bushes, on the hot summer afternoons, when they roamed about in search of amusement; even François himself had often in his childhood played in that very spot, and regaled himself with the tempting fruit growing in such profusion over this hiding-place, little dreaming of the protection which it would one day afford him. With his trusty clasp-knife – the same which had done such good service in severing the leather thong which bound him to his captor, the young Huguenot cut away the branches which impeded his movements, and discovered an aperture, which, although choked up with weeds and rubbish, proved to be what was once the door of the hut. He soon cleared away all obstacles, and creeping through, found himself in the open field, delighted once more to have the free use of his legs.

His first impulse was to make his way to Ferrand's cottage, but when he looked down on his torn and muddy habiliments and saw the scratches on his hands, he felt that if his face was in the same condition he would attract more attention than was desirable; consequently, he thought it more prudent to remain where he was than to run the risk of being recognised by unfriendly eyes. After therefore taking a few brisk turns in front of his novel prison-house, by way of restoring circulation to his benumbed limbs, he determined on re-entering it until nightfall. The poor lad however began to feel the cravings of hunger; there were still some berries on the bushes, but it was late in the season, and they were mostly dried up and withered; so after vainly endeavouring to swallow a few, he gave up the attempt. Thrusting his hands almost petulantly into his pockets, he found a few nuts which he had put there before he left the house the previous evening, and which he had quite forgotten. There were not many, but still these few were a great boon to one who had the moment before fancied he must remain at least another day without food; and creeping back into his place of refuge, he arranged as comfortable a resting-place as he could under the circumstances, and appeased his hunger in some small degree.

Another night closed in, and François Martel, after carefully listening lest any one should be in his way, once more emerged from the ruined hut, and bent his steps to the spot where Jean Ferrand's house stood. His arrival there has been described; and Pierre Hubert, after hearing his recital, proceeded to detail the events of the two previous days. Knowing that his young companion could be trusted, he also unfolded the plans which his master and himself had arranged for the future. Martel at once declared his wish to form one of the party, and Pierre, seeing no objection, acquiesced. 'And now, "mon garçon,"' he exclaimed, 'to bed; we have much to do tomorrow and must be up on time.'

François Martel needed no second bidding, for he was really worn out with fatigue; and throwing himself into one of those strange cupboard looking beds, so frequently to be seen in old French houses, he was soon enjoying a sound sleep; so sound, that he never heard his companion get up the following morning, and had to be awakened more than once, before he could make up his mind to move.

Part of the day was spent in completing the preparations for their journey; and when the sun went down, and their evening meal was over, the two men left the house to go and rejoin those who had preceded them.

Had Pierre Hubert been alone he could have commenced his journey several hours before; his load affording a reason for his undertaking it; but his comrade being a proscribed man, it was necessary to use the utmost caution; and accordingly, they deferred their departure until it was safe for them to venture. François moreover, took the precaution of disguising himself to a certain extent, and providing themselves with stout heavy sticks, they went forth. In due time they reached the place of 'rendezvous,' and had the happiness of meeting Jean Ferrand and his companions, who had arrived thus far in safety.

To The Frontier

Another chapter must be devoted to the further progress of the refugees. The proceeded slowly, and by easy stages to the frontier, and very sorrowful and desponding they would have been, but for the sanguine spirit which animated the young Huguenot, who had so unexpectedly attached himself to their party. It was indeed the best thing which could have happened to them under the circumstances, for Jean Ferrand's grief at the loss of his wife was so great, that, but for his child's sake, he would scarcely have had the energy to take any steps towards making his escape.

This motive however, added to the hopeful suggestions of François, who saw or pretended he saw good in every trifling incident, roused the unhappy man to renewed exertion, even when he was most disinclined for it; and his two servants taking courage from the lad's example, forgot their own trouble, in the desire to cheer their master. True, their spirits were constantly depressed, notwithstanding all their efforts, by what they witnessed during their march – for many and heart rending were the scenes of desolation which met their gaze, as they journeyed onwards – scenes, caused by the unhappy and unjust persecution then raging.

One morning, as they were about to leave the shelter of a wood, they came suddenly upon the ruins of a cottage, which had been so recently burnt down, that smoke was still issuing from the smouldering and charred remains of what had perhaps been, not many hours before, a happy home! It was very early, and none of the peasants who dwelt in the scattered habitations of the neighbourhood were yet stirring; and the utter solitude of the place, the entire absence, so far as they could see, of any living creature whatever, added to the sense of oppressive loneliness, which for the moment weighed down the tired wayfarers. They knew well whose work this was – whose hands had kindled the devouring flames, and instinctively they felt the need of continuing their flight with haste and secrecy.

This spectacle was not, as may be imagined one to allay their fears; on the contrary, it was a powerful incentive to proceed on their journey without delay. But, as they stood for a few moments sadly contemplating the work of destruction before them, and thankfully recognising the mercy which had kept them away from the danger they would inevitably have incurred had they arrived at the spot earlier; they heard a sobbing sound, a sound which had hitherto escaped their notice, and which seemed to come from some person in great distress. It was a childish voice too, which gave utterance to it; and moved to pity by the unmistakable accents of sorrow, they looked cautiously around, just in case they could give some assistance to the afflicted one. François Marcel, with the impetuosity of youth, rushed in the direction whence the sound proceeded, and on the other side of the ruined building, he discovered a girl apparently eight or nine years of age, holding close to her a little boy, who had fallen asleep with his head resting on her lap. She was sitting on a stone, in a dejected attitude, and every now and then tears and sobs would come, as she gazed on the desolation around her. Poor child! She might well weep! For what remained of her home and relations, was centred in the heap of blackened ruins before her, and the little brother who was slumbering near her.

When François approached, she started up with a cry of terror, and looked wildly on the intruder; but his bright honest face at once reassured her, and instead of acting on her first impulse and trying to fly from him, she came up confidingly, and at his invitation followed him to the place where his companions were waiting for him. The little boy, roused from his slumber, clung to his sister in mute astonishment, too young to fear evil, and confiding in her protection.

The surprise of the fugitives on seeing these two children, was great; and many were the questions put and answered, by way of eliciting the reason of the scene of destruction around them. The little girl told them that a party of dragoons had suddenly come upon them the day before. They had attacked the cottagers, and carried off her father, mother, and eldest brother, a boy of twelve years of age, and after setting fire to the place, set off with their prisoners. Her uncle too, who had come to help about some farm-work that day, was amongst the captives. She and her little brother were returning from the wood, where they had been gathering sticks, when all this occurred; and they were so frightened when they heard the shouts of the men and the screams of their mother, and saw the blows which were dealt to them, that they ran away and hid themselves until the noise ceased, and had thus escaped the fate of their relatives.

Jean Ferrand and his friends were now in the greatest perplexity; they looked upon the poor little orphans – for such indeed they were – with profound pity; for there was not the remotest probability of their ever seeing their parents again; they did not know whither they had been carried, and had they done so, never could have found their way to them, alone and helpless

181

as they were. No other habitation appeared near enough for inquiries to be made, as to who would be willing or able to give these poor children an asylum, and it was impossible to leave them to perish from starvation and exposure. Ferrand looked upon his own child; and the remembrance of the protection afforded to him, when in equal peril, pleaded for the forlorn little ones more powerfully perhaps than anything else could have done. A hasty council was therefore called, and after a short deliberation, the little strangers were admitted as members of their party; François Martel volunteering to take them under his own immediate protection, and promising to withdraw with them, if possible, at the approach of danger, in order that the safety of the others might not be endangered.

The children, with the innocence and trustfulness of childhood, followed their kind friends without question, and soon became quite accustomed to their new mode of life. Henri Ferrand rejoiced to have companions with whom he could play when they halted on the march; and Justine Dufrense, and her brother Jules, - who was a quiet delicate child, - learnt ere long to love their little play-fellow dearly.

After many weary days the wanderers reached the frontier, without having met with any hindrance worth recording. Pierre Hubert was obliged to leave them in a place of concealment at some distance from the farm which belonged to his relative, whilst he went to consult with him as to the best means of passing over into a more friendly country. As may be supposed, his companions were in a state of great anxiety during his absence, and the time appeared very long to them. Pierre knew scarcely anything of that part of the country, having only been to visit his cousin once in his life, and that in his early youth; consequently he had been obliged from time to time to ask information as to the road they should follow, always taking care, however, to go alone to the different places where he was obliged to inquire the way; as the appearance of so large a party might create suspicion. With some trouble he found his way to the place he was in search of, and presented himself before his astonished kinsman one afternoon about a fortnight after the beginning of their flight.

The good man welcomed Pierre Hubert heartily; and having heard the purport of his visit, willingly promised his aid in helping the fugitives to escape. He could not hold out any hope that the whole party should be conveyed over the frontier at one time; but he thought that with a little management some of them might be got across in a few days. It would, however, require money to accomplish this, and that Pierre assured him would be forthcoming, Jean Ferrand having both the means and the will to reward any persons who would give him aid in his need, and that he, moreover, was desirous of assisting his fellow-exiles as much as lay in his power.

Having settled matters as far as they could during their interview, it was decided that Pierre Hubert should return to his companions, and bring them to his kinsman's house, as soon as he could do so safely; Joseph Hubert promising them a warm welcome and shelter for as long as he could possibly give it.

The weary travellers in a few hours had again the happiness of being under a friendly roof, and were very thankful for the hospitality of their entertainers. The next day measures were taken for procuring a pass across the frontier for Jean Ferrand, his child, and Jeannette le Roux. The others, it was decided, should remain behind, and join their friends as soon as it would be practicable. Joseph Hubert was successful in his endeavours, and the fugitives, under feigned names, accomplished their perilous journey in safety; Jean Ferrand's gold having proved all powerful, with those who were able to grant them the required permission to pass free. They had to wait some time when once they were across, for the remainder of the party; but at length all were fortunate enough to elude the vigilance of their enemies, and they met once more in deep thankfulness at having so wonderfully effected their escape.

By Ferrand's advice, Pierre and Jeannette were united soon after their arrival in Switzerland. They took Justine Dufrense and her little brother to live with them; and their former master, from his now slender means, managed to contribute something weekly to aid in their support until the poor children were old enough to gain their livelihood. As for himself, he obtained work after a while, and earned sufficient to keep his little household respectably. It required the utmost care and frugality on his part though, so as to enable him to lay by a sufficient sum to defray the expenses of his son's education, when he should be of an age to begin his studies.

Jean Ferrand had dedicated Henri to God's service, and he laboured day after day to give him the learning necessary to become a Pastor of the Reformed Church. The child was still so young, that for some years he cost his father but little; and as he grew older, his devoted parent redoubled his exertions in his behalf, and his labour was blest. He had the unspeakable satisfaction of seeing his beloved Henri grow, little by little, into a high-principled youth, who found favour with each and all who had the happiness of being acquainted with him. At length the father's self-denying care was rewarded; and the day when Henri Ferrand became one of God's appointed ministers, was one of thanksgiving to him, who had toiled so unflinchingly and unremittingly , to obtain his admission to the sacred office. He did not take credit for what he had done; but he thanked his heavenly Father for having permitted him to be the instrument in bringing about the desire of his heart.

Jean Ferrand had now no need to work. It was his son's turn to do so, and cheerfully he shared his all with his father. They lived quietly together in the neighbourhood of Geneva, where they had finally settled. There they often saw their fellow-exiles, for they too had fixed their abode in that beautiful locality, so as to be near him whom they never ceased to look upon as their master, whilst he had learned to call them friends. The greatest pleasure of these worthy people was to sit round the ample hearth on cold winter nights, and, by the red light of the crackling pine logs, which flickered and danced on the walls of the tidy and comfortable living-room, in which it was the custom of that humble household to assemble, to repeat to Henri, their well-beloved Henri, of whom they were so proud, oft-told tales of the land of his birth, - tales of which he never tired of listening to, although he did not remember one single circumstance connected with it. To the older members of the party, the incidents related, tinged as they were with sadness were a never-failing source of pleasure. They loved to recall the scenes where their youth and childhood had been spent, and the friends left behind; when, in those old days of sorrow, they had bidden adieu to their native soil

Yes! It was a pleasure; even to him whose life had been blighted by cruel persecution, which had driven him from his happy home; and he too dwelt fondly on the recollections called up by the friends who had endured so much with him, and for him.

Twenty Years

Twenty years had come and gone, when, one autumn afternoon, a solitary wayfarer might have been seen walking along the road from Toulouse, towards the hamlet where stood the cottage, which belonged to the Bertrands at the time of the furious persecution of the Calvinists. A lull had taken place in the frightful excesses which had been committed in the name of religion; and men had become weary of shedding the blood of their fellow-creatures. Louvois, the cruel and unscrupulous minister of Louis XIV. , was dead, and the Protestants enjoyed a respite from the cruelties and insults which had been heaped upon them. Many exiles had taken advantage of this lull, to revisit their native land; some with the view of re-establishing themselves there, and others only to see once more the homes they had loved so well.

Of the latter number was the lonely traveller who was toiling along the dusty road. He was not an aged man, but he looked older than he really was; his face was thin and careworn, and his scanty locks were of silvery whiteness. He looked like one over whom had swept the storms of life, leaving behind them ineffaceable traces of their ravages. Still, looking at him as he wandered on, lost in thought, one could see that he was 'wearier with heart-sorrows than with the weight of years,' and the same scrutiny also revealed that, whatever griefs he had endured, he had found great peace at the last!

Yes, Jean Ferrand, for it was he who was walking along that familiar road, had learned to be resigned to the will of his heavenly Father, during the years which had passed over his head, and to look forward hopefully to the world beyond the grave. His portion, during a long period of his life, had been one of bitter trial; but, latterly, he had many blessings mingled with his sorrows; and although he never could forget the past, he was more content with the present, and more trusting for the future. Nevertheless, as he advanced on his way, the well-remembered spots which met his gaze on every side, brought back recollections of what had been; the tide of memory rushed through his brain, bringing with it an amount of anguish which he thought had been stilled for ever; and he had need of all his self-control, to hush the feelings, which, in spite of himself, surged up like the waves of the mighty deep, threatening to overwhelm him. He did conquer the repining thoughts however, and after the victory – he had rest! The strife ended, he proceeded on his way; to outward observation calm and composed.

When Jean Ferrand arrived at the hamlet whither he was bound, he saw very little changed there. Some few new cottages had sprung up here and there; but otherwise all was much the same as when he had been there last; the old houses looked older, and that was all; they were so substantially built, that the hand of time, iron though it is, had little power over them, and they looked as if they could stand a good many buffetings from storm and tempest yet. He had therefore little trouble in recognising Gilles Bertrand's house, at the further end of the cluster of dwellings which composed the hamlet. He stopped before it, and knocked for admittance. The door was opened by a pleasant looking girl, who asked him his business; and, on Jean Ferrand's inquiring for the owner of the house, tears came into the girl's eyes, as she answered, that her father was dead. This had happened about ten years before, and her mother, her eldest sister, and herself, had continued to reside in the cottage until about two months since, when her mother died after a short illness. Her sister was married some years before, but she did not survive that event long; she too was taken away suddenly, and Pauline Bertrand was left alone. The death of her mother was the great misfortune of the poor girl's life; she had no one now to whom she could look for advice and help, and she felt her loneliness more than words can express: she said she was trying to reconcile herself to it, and learning to bear her loss with resignation, 'but,' she added, smiling sadly, 'it takes sometime to do that.'

None knew better than Jean Ferrand how impossible it is to forget the past, and how difficult it is to submit without complaint, when God sees fit to withdraw what we have held most dear. He had passed through that fiery trial himself, and felt irresistibly drawn towards the poor orphan now standing before him. Taking her hand in his, he told her who he was, and why he had returned to France; adding, that he could not pass the door of those who had shown him so much kindness in the time of his sorest need, without stopping to inquire for them.

Pauline – the little Pauline of years gone by – was greatly astonished at this announcement; she expressed great pleasure at seeing him again; she remembered him slightly, more probably as being connected with the little boy who had so unexpectedly become an inmate of their dwelling on the eventful evening before described; and she told him how often he, and the child so miraculously rescued by her mother, had been recalled to the memory of them by her parents. She invited Jean Ferrand into the house, telling him he must make it his home during his stay in that part of the country: and placing refreshments before him, very acceptable after his long march, she went to prepare his room. Right glad was the tired man to find such a resting-place, and he was soon quite at home with his young hostess. There was a charming simplicity about Pauline that went straight to the old man's heart, and took it completely by storm; and he had not been with her long, before he came to a very important decision concerning her. A few evenings after his arrival he told her, as they were sitting on the stone bench outside the house – the bench he had such good reason to remember, - that the dearest wish of his heart was to take her to his distant home in Switzerland. 'You know, Pauline,' said he, 'that under Providence I am indebted to your mother for the restoration of my child; and with his restoration, to the possession of more happiness than I had ever dreamed it possible I should enjoy in this world again; let me, my child, repay that debt of gratitude to her, by adopting you as my daughter. '

Pauline Bertrand raised her large dark eyes to his, and saw how earnest he was in offering her a home. The thought of having some one to care for, and who would be a protector to her in years to come, was very grateful to the orphan's feelings; and she saw a vista of happiness opening before her, which seemed almost too great to be real. Her gentle nature yearned for companionship, and she listened to the pleadings of her own heart, as much perhaps as to the words of her old friend when she replied, 'Oh! Monsieur Ferrand! You are indeed too good; can it be possible that such a blessing is in store for me? You know I have no near relations; no one who would or could take me in, should sickness overtake me, and oh! I am indeed very lonely! Surely God guided your steps hither, Monsieur Ferrand?'

'Aye! My child, His hand leads us everywhere, and deeply thankful am I to Him for having put it into my heart to come here. You will return with me, Pauline?' The kind tones of the old man's voice brought tears into the eyes of his young companion, but not tears of sorrow, although they for a moment choked her utterance. When she had controlled her emotion sufficiently to reply, she said, while a faint smile illuminated her features, 'Yes! I will go with you; that is, if I may; but I should wish to consult one or two old friends on the subject; I should not like to undertake so momentous a thing, without due consideration and advice. '

'By all means, my child! Neither would I wish you to undertake so important a step hurriedly or inadvisably, it would not be seemly; ask therefore the opinion of those on whose judgment you can rely, and take time before you decide; I shall await your decision. '

It was so settled, and the next few days were devoted to making the necessary arrangements; for Pauline met with little opposition, or even discouragement, when she communicated her wishes to the friend she had thought it best to consult. It so happened that those whose advice she asked had a secret leaning for the Calvinist form of worship, although they, from dread of the consequences, still adhered to the Romish faith; they moreover had no special interest in keeping this young girl amongst them, and perhaps foresaw that if they prevented her accompanying her old friend, she might eventually remain on their hands, and in the event of her becoming incapable of working for her livelihood, the responsibility of providing for her maintenance would, in all probability, devolve on them. The decision being left to Pauline, she did not keep Jean Ferrand long in suspense. Joyfully did he receive the intelligence, that his offer of adoption was accepted, and some days were passed in making preparations for the journey. The house and furniture were let to a neighbour, who had long wished to inhabit it, and all other less important matters were satisfactorily arranged. At length the day of their departure was fixed. On the previous evening, the young girl and her adopted father walked along the banks of the river for the last time. It was a quiet walk, and both were very silent, for their thoughts were busy with the past. Together they visited the last resting-place of those they had loved and lost, and each prayed that God would re-unite them in that blessed place, where there are no sorrows or partings, and where all tears are wiped away.

It is not necessary to follow them on their journey, it is enough to say that they reached home in safety. Sometime afterwards Pauline Bertrand became to Henri Ferrand what Louise Derval had been to his father, a fond and devoted wife. Her pleasant winning ways won the hearts of all; even Jeannette, who was known to say that there was no one quite good enough to be her beloved young master's wife, could find no fault with his choice, and she soon learned to love Pauline for her own sake.

It will be asked how a Roman Catholic could marry a Reformer? That certainly was a stumbling-block at first; but little by little the young girl's religious opinions had been shaken by the teaching and example of those, with whom she came in daily contact. More and more did she appreciate the lessons taught by men who had endured pain and hardship; nay, had faced death itself rather than give up the belief of their consciences; and with her admiration for the doctrines which they inculcated, came the conviction, that her own faith fell far short of theirs. Pauline, therefore, in the end became a willing convert to the creed of the Huguenots, and remained ever after a faithful member of that much maligned and persecuted branch of the Church.

Her young husband blessed the day when his father had persuaded the orphan to become his adopted daughter; and she, oh! How unutterably thankful did she feel to the merciful Providence which had prompted Jean Ferrand to make the proposal. Henri and his wife lived together many years; they reared a numerous family of sons and daughters, and closed the eyes of their beloved father, when the angel of death summoned him from his earthly home, to inherit the portion reserved for those whom God loves, and those who love Him.

Before we take leave of these good people, we must say a few words about the humble friends who had accompanied them into exile.

Justine Dufrense, now grown into a tall comely woman, went to live with Henri and Pauline Ferrand at the time of their marriage. Up to that period she had resided with Pierre Hubert and his wife, and was to them as a daughter; but when young Henri, asked as a favour that Justine should come and help his bride in her household duties, they joyfully gave their consent. Little Jules had died about two years after their arrival in Switzerland; he had been a delicate child and his health, impaired by fatigue and privation, and by the chilling influence of the atmosphere of his adopted country, soon gave way entirely, and, notwithstanding the loving care bestowed upon him, he gradually faded away, and was laid in his little grave by his sorrowing friends.

Justine did not remain long with Monsieur and Madame Ferrand. About a year after she had taken up her abode with them, François Martel claimed the fulfilment of a promise, made some years before. This promise was, that she should become his wife whenever he had a home to offer her. He was now in a position to do so. When he arrived in Switzerland he decided on learning a trade; he was still young enough to do so, and by his application and industry soon mastered the difficulties he met with. Being high principled and well conducted, he gained the esteem and confidence of those who employed him; one of these, a well-to-do citizen, having a small cottage at his disposal, offered it to François and allowed him to live in it at a nominal rent, at the same time keeping him well supplied with work; and into this cottage he brought Justine Dufrense on their wedding day. Henri Ferrand united them in marriage, as pastor of a little flock of Reformers, who had congregated in the pleasant spot where he now dwelt, and it added to the happiness of François and Justine that their young master had given them his benediction on that eventful day.

We have now done with the fortunes of Jean Ferrand and his friends, and must return to the others in this true tale; leaving the exiles in the enjoyment of peace and contentment, in the land which they had chosen for their abiding place.

A Martyr's Death

We must now go back to the time when we first became acquainted with the events described in the last few chapters, and take up our narrative on the morning when Pastor Morin accompanied Monsieur d'Aureville to Toulouse as a prisoner. The day had not yet dawned, when they left the house where the old man had rested after the funeral of Louise Ferrand; but it was not a dark night, and as the captor and his captive rode on side by side conversing freely, they could see the long straight road before them distinctly. The young officer, during that ride, learned much about the Huguenots, which he had not previously known. He had never believed the absurd reports which some of their Roman Catholic brethren so diligently circulated about them; his mind was too unprejudiced to put any faith in idle tales, such as were repeated from time to time; but he never had the opportunity until now of hearing from the lips of an educated member of the Reformed Church, an account of opinions held by that portion of his fellow-subjects. He listened therefore with deep interest to the explanations which the Reformer gave him, of the difference between his religion and theirs; and as he listened, he unconsciously became impressed with the conviction, that those who had abjured the errors of the Romish faith were serving God more perfectly, than those who persecuted and reviled them.

He had happily fallen in with a man who was capable of giving him a true insight into the real state of the case; one, who although no bigot, was a truly pious and devoted Christian; one of those shining lights, who now and again are given to the world as bright examples to those over whom they are appointed ministers. He was a learned, eloquent, and humble-minded man, as has been elsewhere said; and the simple narration of the sufferings endured by the poor persecuted members of his afflicted Church, won from his companion heartfelt commiseration; and he resolved to do all in his power to help the unfortunate prisoners to escape the sad fate impending over them.

When they arrived at Toulouse, Monsieur Morin and Armand d'Aureville were obliged to part. The latter, having fulfilled the task appointed to him, had nothing more to do with his prisoner; but, he left him with the promises to interest himself in his favour, and in that of the other unfortunates who had been captured. He accordingly – after seeing the aged pastor consigned to the cell which was in readiness for him – went with as little delay as possible to the house of Monsieur d'Aubigny, his intended father-in-law, whose home was in that city. Monsieur d'Aubigny entertained very favourable impressions with regard to the Reformed faith, although he was still a Roman Catholic, and he readily promised the aid implored by Armand d'Aureville. He immediately went to offer his services as the legal adviser of the unhappy prisoners, and undertook their defence with a courage beyond words to express. He knew that every sentence he uttered might be turned to his own destruction; but he spared not his arguments, he implored, he entreated, he appealed to the consciences of the judges who sat on that iniquitous trial, in words of untold eloquence; but he appealed in vain; the hearts of those men were made of stone, and an angel from heaven would have failed to convince them. They had one amongst them who incited them to the commission of every evil deed, under the plea of loyalty to their country and their God, and all bowed down before that arch-deceiver. Yes! Father Anselmo was there, triumphant! What wonder then, that good men and true, - for there were some few yet among those appointed to judge their fellow-men on this unhappy day, - what wonder then they were forced to yield the palm to him, who equally learned and more subtle, was more than a match for them. His wily words, and his unscrupulous conscience, carried him through difficulties, which more single-minded men could not overcome. He gained his point, and his victims were ruined!

During the trial he recognised Monsieur Morin, and with the recognition came the remembrance of Suzanne de l'Orme. He took an early opportunity of questioning the good man as to what had become of her, forgetting in his eagerness to regain possession of her, his usual caution. A look of joy and thankfulness passed over the venerable pastor's face, as he heard the question, and he involuntarily exclaimed, 'Then she has escaped! The Lord be praised for this unexpected mercy!'

Father Anselmo started; for once in his life he had been thrown off his guard, and had spoken inadvisably. He ground his teeth in his fury, and glared vindictively at the venerable man before him. He would willingly have recalled the words of comfort he had unthinkingly uttered, but it was not in his power to do so, and he only hated his opponent with a more bitter hatred, that he had imparted a gleam of sunshine to the last hours of his sorrowful existence.

Time went on, and the trial which had occupied many days, was at length ended. Sentence was passed, and each knew their doom. Some were condemned to imprisonment of longer or shorter duration, according as their offence had been judged; others were publicly scourged, - women there were amongst these — aye! Incredible though it may seem, - women were subjected to that cruel indignity, and they bore their punishment with the courage of martyrs! One, - the rash and unhappy author of this terrible calamity, - Monsieur de la Ferriére, was broken alive on the wheel, in the great square of the city; and, whatever fault he may have committed in his mistaken zeal, by inducing his fellow-sufferers to transgress the laws of the kingdom, it certainly was in a good cause; and he expiated his error with the greatest fortitude, and bore unheard of sufferings with a calmness so heroic, that even his tormentors could not but pause in involuntary admiration.

Monsieur Morin's doom was equally fearful! The faggot and the stake were his portion; and he too, endured his punishment with a meekness and courage beyond compare, with his last breath asserting his innocence of the crimes imputed to him, and praying for mercy on the deluded fanatics who were torturing him. By the special intervention of the Governor of the province, who was a humane man and a gentleman, the good pastor was allowed to visit his unhappy brethren, before they suffered; and his exhortations and prayers smoothed the rough and thorny path which most of them had to tread. The same indulgent hand granted permission to Monsieur d'Aubigny and Armand d'Aureville, to visit their aged friend whenever they felt disposed to do so; and they availed themselves of that permission with thankfulness. The lessons of holiness they learned during their prison visits were such as never to be forgotten in after years; and formed the subject of conversation and instruction to their children and their children's children, long after the spirit of him who had uttered them had passed away.

The last day of Monsieur Morin's life on earth had dawned, and attended by his faithful friends he went to the place of execution. Yes! Those friends whom he had found in the hour of adversity remained steadfast to the end. They thought not of their own feelings on this awful occasion, they repressed the agony which they knew they must endure in seeing the torture inflicted on a helpless being, and one too, who had in no way deserved such a punishment; and they marked their sense of his worth, at the risk of their lives, by going with him to his doom, and sustaining him by their presence and sympathy, in his extremity. It was in truth a solemn and fearful spectacle, which the 'Grand Place,' at Toulouse, presented on that day! Thousands upon thousands had assembled there, it being the place appointed for the sacrifice; and, filled to overflowing as the large space already was, crowds of men and women still hurried thither, pushing and jostling each other, in the hope of obtaining a glimpse of the terrible proceedings. Most of the windows in the houses surrounding that great square were occupied by anxious expectant persons who waited there patiently for a chance of seeing the death-agonies of him who was about to suffer. Processions of priests paraded the streets on their way to the fatal spot; some of those priests caring little to repress the exultation they felt at the triumph about to be obtained over one whom they considered an arch-heretic; whilst others, more enlightened, and it may be, mercifully inclined and better Christians, deploring the cruelty of the act, could not, if they would, withdraw from playing their part in the unholy pageant.

Troops too, marched past, ranging themselves around the fatal pile, so as to frustrate any insane attempt on the part of the Huguenots to rescue the condemned man, who was justly regarded by them as one of the most devoted champions of their faith. The appointed hour having arrived, Monsieur Morin was conducted to his place of doom, and he ascended the lofty place where he was to expiate his supposed offences. The multitude heaved and swayed about, as if impatient for the fearful tragedy to begin; and the aged pastor gazed for some moments with the deepest commiseration on the sea of upturned faces below him; he knew they were thirsting for his blood, but he prayed for them, and contemplated his fate unmoved. His hope was anchored on

199

the Rock of Ages; what could harm him now? Certainly not the storm and fury of bad men's passions; not the pain, which, though excruciating, 'endureth but for a moment. ' The fire was kindled – the flames shot upwards, and when the smoke cleared away, the old man's face was seen wearing a smile which could only have been reflected from heaven – and so he passed from death unto life, even life everlasting; and his ransomed spirit was enrolled in the ranks of the noble army of martyrs; for ever freed from trouble, persecution, and woe!

France, unhappy France! Bitterly in after days didst thou reap the fruit of the iniquities committed in those days; when thy best and noblest blood had been wantonly shed, and thy true-hearted sons driven from thy shores; when whose evil-minded ones, who had sown the seeds of wickedness amongst the corrupted masses of thy infatuated people, perpetrated crimes even more fearful than these; and made thy name a bye-word among nations. Let us now take leave of thee; for with the death of Monsieur Morin, our connection with the land of his birth ceases.

LAND IN SIGHT

We must now follow in the wake of the vessel which is ploughing the deep, freighted with so many cares and sorrows. Most of the little band who had found refuge on board from the rage and tyranny of their enemies, bore a load of anxiety as to the future, which nothing but a firm trust in the help of the Almighty could have enabled them to bear.

Pierre de l'Orme, as he paced the deck thoughtfully could not prevent his mind from reverting to the past and contrasting it with the present. He had great misgivings as to whether his child would eventually recover the health which had been so cruelly and wantonly destroyed. He had also not been able to obtain any portion of his property, as he had hoped to do; his visit to his native land having been of so secret a nature, that any attempt on his part to obtain restitution would have marked him out for destruction. The wants of his family were comparatively few, but his children were growing up, and if it pleased God to spare them, they must be educated and set up in life. How was he to do this with his narrowed means? He pondered over his trouble day by day, and grew more despondent as time went on. The demeanour of the Huguenot was at all times grave, but now a gloom and sadness seemed to have settled on his countenance, which no effort on the part of his fellow-travellers was able to dissipate.

On the particular day of which we now write, he appeared unusually depressed. The day had been intensely hot; but as it drew to a close a fresh and pleasant breeze had sprung up, very acceptable to our voyagers, all unused as they were to the small compass and restraint, which most of them for the first time in their lives were compelled to endure. The burning rays of the sun had obliged them to remain down below the greater part of the day; and the atmosphere of the cabin had been almost suffocating. They had now assembled on deck to breathe the pure air; and the light breeze which was now filling their sails, and accelerating the speed of the ship, seemed to impart a shade of colour to the pale cheek of Suzanne, as she lay there supported on cushions. Her kind friend Jeanne le Grand sat by her side, ready to give her any assistance she might require, for the poor child was very helpless. The invigorating sea air, it is true, had been of great use; it kept up the little strength she had. Victor, the merry good-tempered Victor, had been amusing her with tales of by-gone days, which had interested her much, and occasionally her sweet happy laugh fell on her father's ear like far off music.

It was evening, and the sun was sinking lower and lower, in a perfect blaze of glory. Gold, purple, and crimson, seemed striving with each other for supremacy in the glorious vault of heaven, whilst along the horizon the ever restless waves reflected the gorgeous colouring of the clouds above. Overhead the azure sky was gradually deepening in hue, the evening star peeped out in her pale beauty, and seemed placed there as a beacon to the toil-worn and sorrow-stricken; suggesting thoughts of that 'better land,' where strife and care are unknown. As eventide, with its calm peacefulness, stole in upon that little world, the sailors hushed their usual noisy talk, as if feeling the quieting spell of that pleasant hour; and even Pierre de l'Orme's gloomy thoughts and forebodings took a brighter colouring from the peaceful beauty of the scene around him. With a deep sigh he turned to where his little daughter lay surrounded by her friends; his countenance wearing a more hopeful look as he said, 'Well, my Suzanne, how are you feeling this evening?'

'Better, dear Father! Certainly better! If I could only see you looking happy and cheerful, I think I should get quite well very soon.'

'Ah! My child,' replied her father, 'it is not easy to look cheerful with such a weigh of anxiety on my mind; the future does not wear a very encouraging aspect, Suzanne!'

'Alas, no, dear Father; but it is such a blessing to have escaped from our cruel enemies, and to have the prospect of being all re-united in a home which we will make happy for each other; is it not so?'

'Yes, my child! I feel deeply thankful for all the mercies which have been vouchsafed to us; but, you cannot understand what my fears are with regard to the means I shall have of bringing up my children. You know that in this unjust persecution I must now depend on my own exertions for the maintenance of my family. If God gives me health and strength, all will be well: but . . .'

'Oh! Father; "God will provide;" you know you have often impressed that on our minds before the trouble came; when we used to talk of what happened, and feel afraid, you would say, "My children, do not fear, God will provide!" Have you forgotten?'

Tears stood in Monsieur de l'Orme's eyes, and as he stooped down to kiss his child, he whispered, 'you are right, Suzanne; henceforth I shall cast all my care upon Him.'

At this moment the captain came up, and said, that if the wind continued for some hours longer in the same quarter, he hoped to reach the shores of England on the morrow. This announcement was heard with unfeigned satisfaction by all; for although their voyage had been a prosperous one, they began to weary of its monotony. Gladly, therefore, they hailed the promise made by Capitaine la Croix, and they separated for the night with mutual congratulations on the prospect of so speedily being released from what was little better than imprisonment to some of them.

On the evening of the next day they came in sight of land, and early the following morning disembarked. Slow and fatiguing was the journey to London, but at last the great city was reached, and the little party, almost worn out with fatigue, arrived at the house occupied by Monsieur de l'Orme and his family.

LONGING FOR NEWS

L et us now take a peep at Madeleine de l'Orme, as she sits day after day longing for news of her husband and child. When first our story opened, we found her oppressed with grief and anxiety, but comely and well attired, and with her matronly beauty still undimmed. Now, months of wearying incertitude have passed over that fair head, and left many a silver thread in the luxuriant masses of her soft brown hair. Let us look at her now, occupied as she is, much in the same manner as when we first saw her on that sultry July afternoon, when she was waiting for her husband's return; and let us mark the difference.

Madame de l'Orme is much, very much paler and thinner, than in those old days; there is a look of care on her expressive countenance, which tells of sorrow – sorrow which, however meekly borne, has left some traces where it has passed. On the afternoon we write, she is sitting in a small scantily furnished room on the ground floor of a house in a quiet London street. This street was not exactly a thoroughfare, and was, in those far off days, almost like the country for quietness; few people passed along its grass-grown pavement, and the advent of a vehicle of any sort was almost unknown. The houses in this street were mostly inhabited by persons of small means; people who preferred this solitary neighbourhood to the more lively and expensive parts of London.

The room in which Madeleine de l'Orme pursued her homely household task was neat and well kept; but there was no superfluity of furniture in it, for her husband's means had not yet been great enough to admit of their purchasing anything which was not positively needful. It was however, as comfortable as a person of her orderly habits could make it; and as she sits there, one could well fancy her the presiding genius of the place; she could have sustained that character in both cottage and palace; and acted as well in one as in the other. Now, her silken garments and costly laces have been laid aside, and her garb is one more suited to her altered fortunes; but she needs no ornament to enhance the natural grace of her appearance, and notwithstanding her care-worn looks, Madeleine de l'Orme is beautiful still. Two of her children are in the room with her. Marie, sitting on a low stool at her feet, is busy with some piece of work suitable to a child of her years. Her round blue eyes are from time to time fixed wonderingly on her mother's sad face; without, however, venturing to ask the cause of a sorrow she could not comprehend. Jean is seated at a table absorbed in the studies which his father had marked out for him before his departure; -studies which he had scrupulously attended to, knowing the pleasure it would give his father on his return, to find his wishes had been carried out.

Jean had grown very much since the day he left his beloved home in France. The graces of his mind had kept pace with those of his person; and his kindly, warm-hearted disposition endeared him to every one with whom he came in contact. His fresh rosy face indicated health; and the sparkle of his blue eyes reminded one strongly of what his mother's had been before sorrow had dimmed their lustre. Yes! Jean de l'Orme was a noble-looking boy, and one of whom his parents might well be proud. His intellectual abilities were of no mean order; and he was fitting himself, if God so willed it, to help his father in the arduous labours which adverse fortune imposed on him. Added to all this, he possessed an honest and true heart, and would have scorned to do a mean or underhand action. He was dressed in the quaint manner of the times, in a suit of russet brown; his nether garments fastened at the knee with small silver buckles, his stockings of the same hue as his dress, and his high-heeled untanned leather boots adorned with large rosettes of silk. His hair, of a more golden shade of brown than his mother's was dressed as was customary for children occupying the same station in life as he did. It was combed down straight, to within an inch of his eye-brows, and on the sides and at the back of his head, it fell in heavy masses of shining curls, over a large linen collar edged with lace. This collar was turned over his doublet, and nearly reached his shoulders; it was fastened by a bunch of bright coloured ribbon, leaving his finely formed throat exposed, and relieving his otherwise sombre attire.

As they sit thus pursuing their different occupations a deep sigh from his mother attracted Jean de l'Orme's attention, and looking up from his book, he saw the tears silently coursing each other down her pale cheeks, as with tightly clasped hands she leaned back in her chair. In an instant he was by her side, lavishing every endearment on her, and trying all in his power to calm her agitation. For a time his efforts were vain; he did not ask what ailed her, for he knew but too well what were the thoughts which had caused her tears to flow; and sending his little sister out of the room, he took her place at his mother's feet, and tried to soothe the grief he could not cure, by suggesting hopes, which with the buoyancy of youth he still entertained, as to the return

207

of his father and their darling Suzanne. Madame de l'Orme was more depressed this day than usual. She was not strong; and she felt most keenly the truth of the proverb, that 'hope deferred maketh the heart sick;' and as she pondered over the protracted absence of her husband, and his long silence, she felt that if this suspense lasted much longer, her life or her reason would fail; and she never would enjoy the happiness she had so long pined for.

Whilst Monsieur de l'Orme had been absent poor Madeleine had had a long and expensive illness, from which she was only just recovering. A little child had been born soon after her husband's departure, and after being her joy and comfort for a few days, God had seen fit to take him back. The little flower drooped in this cold world, and its heavenly Father transplanted it into His glorious garden. There the chill blasts of adversity could never reach him, and he was for ever safe from the storms which assail those whom He appoints to do battle with the world, its trials and temptations. Madeleine de l'Orme, in her weakness, could not at first see the mercy of God in this bereavement; she felt as if she must sink under the weight of her great sorrows, and a complete prostration of her energies was the consequence. The long illness which followed had almost drained her slender purse; and she often, as on this day, pined for the return of him who, in all things temporal, was her comfort and stay. She, however, did not forget to bring her cares and griefs to Him, who is able and willing to heal the wounds which in His wisdom He sees fit to inflict; and as her strength returned, she less often gave way to such depression as now assailed her. After a time she listened calmly to the suggestions of her boy, as to the probable reasons for the delay in his father's return.

They conversed for some time, and she had quite recovered her composure, when during a pause in their conversation, that attention of each was arrested by the sound of footsteps echoing on the pavement of the half deserted street. 'Jean,' exclaimed Madame de l'Orme, starting up, 'it is your father's step!' In an instant the boy was on his feet, and intently listening to the sound which had caused his mother's exclamation. Nearer and nearer it approached; Madeleine, with blanched cheek and palpitating heart, waited in agonising suspense for the confirmation of her hopes. Nearer and nearer came the sound, and other footsteps besides the well-known one became audible; then there was a hush, and voices were heard as if in consultation; then again a single footstep approached the house, and Madeleine's heart almost stood still, as she more fully recognised the sound she knew so well. In a few moments her hopes were realized, and she was clasped in her husband's arms; his loved voice sounded in her ears, but she hardly understood her great happiness yet, for her mind was occupied with the thought of her lost child. Terror lest she should be told to hope no more held her tongue enchained; and she could only look the questions she could not articulate.

There had been no means of apprizing Madame de l'Orme of her husband's enterprise; and he justly dreaded the effect Suzanne's altered appearance would have upon her mother. He therefore bade the others wait outside with her, until he could prepare his poor Madeleine for the sight which would greet her loving eyes; and well he did so, for the length and fatigue of the land journey had undone what the quiet of the sea voyage had effected; and the child was reduced to the greatest weakness, by the time she reached her home.

At length all was told; and Pierre de l'Orme brought in his daughter, and laid her in his wife's arms. The emotion of this long coveted meeting proved too strong for the child; and uttering faintly, 'Oh! My mother!' She lost all consciousness of what was passing around her. The children stood, looking on in awe, at the sister whom they did not recognise in the changed and faded being now lying in their mother's arms. Jean alone, old enough to feel that it must be indeed his own Suzanne, wept silently; and kissed, without ceasing, the wasted hands now lying powerless by her side.

And what of Madeleine? The poor grief-stricken Madeleine? She neither spoke nor wept; but as she gazed on her first-born, she felt that ere long she would have another child in heaven; but even in that hour of anguish, her heart was lifted to God in her wordless agony; and He heard the unuttered prayer form strength to give up to Him the long lost treasure so lately found.

Yes! Madeleine de l'Orme, the Christian mother, could even then submit her will to that of Him, who, she knew, did not afflict her willingly; and although her cheek grew paler and paler, and her lip quivered with irrepressible emotion, she whispered to her husband that she felt 'all would be well,' and implored him, for the sake of the dear child now lying in her arms, to bear patiently the cross which was weighing so heavily on them.

Meanwhile old Marthe had been busy supplying restoratives, with the assistance of Jeanne le Grand; and, ere long they had the satisfaction of seeing Suzanne return to consciousness. She opened her eyes, and gazed anxiously round at the sorrowful faces of her relatives; and smiling faintly, said in a voice above a whisper, 'Thank God for bringing me home again!' Then turning towards her mother, she added, 'Oh, mother! I am so weary, take me to my bed. '

Very tenderly was she laid upon the couch, which was at once prepared for her, and on that couch she remained for many months, a weak and helpless invalid. She was tended by loving friends, and all that mortal could do to alleviate her suffering, was done. For a long time her life was despaired of, and her parents feared their precious Suzanne would not be spared to them; then, when all hope was well-nigh gone, God's mercy was extended to the patient child; and her sufferings gradually decreased.

For many weeks the debility consequent on her illness compelled her to remain in her bed; but at last the kind physician who had attended her from the time of her arrival, and who was the father of one of Monsieur de l'Orme's pupils, gave her permission to leave it, and mix once more with the beloved ones, who were so anxious to welcome her amongst them; and Suzanne de l'Orme arose from her sick-bed, restored comparatively to health and strength. But alas! She was hopelessly deformed. The heavy burdens she had borne had not only stunted her growth, but had caused such a distortion of her spine, that no treatment, however skilful, could ever remedy or even conceal the deformity; and so she remained to the end of her life, a monument of the cruelty of man.

Who shall describe the feelings of her father, - of her gentle loving mother? Outwardly they remained calm; each, for the sake of the other, tried to conceal the grief which consumed them; and after a while God blessed their unselfish endeavours, and they enjoyed 'that peace which the world cannot give, neither can it take away. ' Suzanne herself, by her sweetness and cheerfulness, did much to reconcile them to see her deformed for the remainder of her days; and when sometimes her mother, fancying herself unobserved, would gaze at her with tears in her eyes, as the poor girl moved awkwardly about the room, she would say caressingly, 'you are not grieving for me, are you, mother? I am very happy as I am! How happy I can never describe. Is it not inexpressible joy to be once more at home with you all, when I had almost lost all hope of seeing you again in this world? And who knows, dear mother, I might perhaps have grown vain of my beauty, if this trial had not been sent to remind me of the sinfulness of being so. Ah! Depend upon it, all is right as it is,' – and then, she added seriously, 'in heaven there will be no difference between me and the others, if I bear my cross meekly and without complaint on earth; pray for me then, my own mother, that strength may be given me to bear whatever it is God's pleasure to order. '

Thus Suzanne consoled her mother, and by degrees she became more reconciled to see her darling's altered appearance. By her brothers and sisters she was almost idolized, - they consulted her in all their little difficulties; their pleasures ceased to be such, if she shared not in them – and in their childish quarrel, Suzanne was always the peace-maker. 'Ah!' She used to say on such occasions, 'do not speak angrily to one another, you know not how soon it may please God to separate you, and then you will be sorry; if, like me, you had been many months without ever seeing the face of a child, you would never feel inclined to say an angry word to one another. ' She would then soothe their ruffled tempers, and invariably reconcile the little disputants. She was indeed a blessing to them all; her modesty and meekness were her safeguard, otherwise she would perhaps have been tempted, as many other children of her age would have been – her temper might have been spoilt by the indulgence she received; and she might have been overbearing and exacting. Suzanne, however, was not an ordinary child; her early trials had sowed the seeds of many rare virtues, which advancing years matured into perfection; and thus she lived, in singleness of heart, fearing God, and doing her duty in the state of life which He had appointed for her.

The remainder of Suzanne de l'Orme's life was uneventful. She had many difficulties to contend with; and her sensitive mind often suffered from the incautious remarks of thoughtless individuals; she soon, however, recovered the calmness momentarily disturbed, and would endeavour to find excuses for those who inflicted the pain.

As Suzanne grew up to womanhood she was her mother's great comfort, assisting her in her household duties, and the care of the younger children. Monsieur de l'Orme's family had to undergo many privations, which had been undreamt of in the old happy days before they left their beloved France. It was many years before he could realize, by his exertions, sufficient to defray the expenses of his children's education; and they all had to exercise the strictest economy, so as to keep up their little establishment in the respectability which they had always been accustomed to. After a time his earnest endeavours were blessed, and having succeeded in recovering some portion of his fortune, he was enabled to relax his arduous labours, and take the rest he so much needed.

As Monsieur de l'Orme's children grew up, they each settled in homes of their own, with the exception of Suzanne and Jean, who both remained to be the comfort of their parent's declining years. Jean had a disappointment in his early youth; he had sought and won the affections of an amiable young girl, the daughter of refugees like themselves, and their union was sanctioned by both families; but, a little time before the marriage was to have taken place, Adéle de la Chesnaye was seized with a mortal illness, and in a few weeks was laid in her grave. Jean de l'Orme mourned for her sincerely, and the place she had occupied in his affections was never filled up; but, as time passed, the poignancy of his sorrow was alleviated; and he once more took his place in his father's house, a sadder man, but one who accepted the decree of an unerring providence, in the true Christian spirit of resignation. He assisted his father in instructing his pupils; and to Suzanne he was a pleasant and loving companion. His respect for his sister almost amounted to veneration; and he would relate her early trials and extraordinary fortitude, as almost unique. He was the devoted champion of his beloved and afflicted sister in his youth; and in his manhood he was her stay and support, long after their parents had ceased to exist.

A SECRET LOVE

We must, ere we conclude, say a few words about the le Grands, those tried friends whom no ill-fortune could change. Jeanne remained with the de l'Orme's for several months, whilst her brothers went about seeking employment suitable to their ability and former experience. A long time they were unsuccessful; for, having no knowledge of the English language, except the few words they had picked up since their arrival, they found great difficulty in making their wishes intelligible; and they were beginning to despair, when one day they accidentally met their old friend Capitaine la Croix. He had just returned from a short voyage, and had come up to London to dispose of his cargo.

This was a pleasant meeting on both sides, for the worthy sailor was anxious to see his friends, in order to impart the success of his undertaking; and they were equally delighted to see him for various other reasons. In the first place, the ready money they had brought with them was gradually diminishing; and they had misgivings as to their being able to obtain employment in England, even as farm labourers. Other work was totally unsuited to them, who had from their earliest youth been accustomed to agricultural pursuits; they therefore hailed their countrymen's advent with unfeigned delight; and were soon listening with intense pleasure to a scheme which la Croix proposed for their consideration.

He had just returned from one of those islands on the coast of Normandy, which, although so close to the shores of France as to seem part and parcel of it, are nevertheless the undisputed property of the Sovereigns of England. They are the remnant of that fair Duchy which the Conqueror possessed before he invaded Britain. These islands had been but little known, but in the previous reign Jersey, the largest of them, had afforded shelter to England's fugitive Sovereign; and in gratitude for services and kindnesses received at the hands of the islanders, Charles II granted them charters and privileges which they enjoy to this day. Little by little, as navigation improved, the Norman isles were visited by English mariners; and thus it came to pass that Capitaine la Croix, having heard of these islands, where the language of his native land was spoken and understood, made up his mind to make a voyage there.

Having succeeded beyond his expectations, he described to his delighted auditors what he had seen and done; and had little trouble in persuading them to go and try their fortune in one of those islands. Jeanne le Grand had, of course to be consulted; her consent, however, was not difficult to obtain; more especially when she was told that numbers of French refugees had found a home there. Accordingly, as soon as their preparations were made, they set sail from London; and after a prosperous voyage, arrived at their destination.

It matters little which of the islands they selected for their resting-place; enough if we say, that after a time the brothers were in a position to purchase a small farm, which they cultivated successfully. Victor married and had a family; but Paul and his sister remained single, and lived to a good old age. Jeanne never saw her friends the de l'Orme's again; but her brothers more than once went to England in some trading vessel, and never without some substantial remembrance to their less fortunate fellow-exiles.

It was a matter of surprise to many, that Paul le Grand never married, for he was a fine looking man, and singularly gifted for one in his station; but he, like many others, could have told a tale of hopes never to be realized. None ever suspected that the grave thoughtful man, who lived so quietly with his sister, had ever had a wish beyond that home fireside; and yet it was so! Paul le Grand had visions of happiness with one, who, to her dying day, never knew the affection she had inspired; for he never ventured by word or look to tell the love which he felt was hopeless. He died before his sister; and after his death, as she and Victor were examining his effects, one small discoloured piece of paper, neatly folded, was found in his old fashioned pocket book; it was inscribed with the single word 'Suzanne,' and contained a lock of dark silken hair. Jeanne at once recognised it as having belonged to her – she had missed it, and searched for it in vain, till one day, mentioning her loss before Paul, she had noticed a peculiar expression on his face; and with a woman's tact changed the subject. She guessed her brother's secret, and respected it. As they advanced in years, she had forgotten the circumstance; and it was only when she saw this little token, which had been a parting gift from her young favourite at her own earnest request, that the remembrance of what had occurred returned to her memory.

Tears dimmed the eyes of the affectionate brother and sister at this proof of silent and uncomplaining suffering; and they remembered many a sigh and yearning look which had then passed without notice on the part of one, or comment from the other. Their beloved brother was now at rest, and it mattered little for the shadow which had been cast on his earthly existence; they were fully aware that he had not allowed that shadow to interfere with his duties, but had gone on bravely, making others happy, and endeavouring to be so himself, notwithstanding the weight which often lay on his heart. In his visits to London he always saw Suzanne de l'Orme, but he never let her suspect his feelings towards her. The difference in their rank was too great for him to risk a refusal; and although her virtues had made an unalterable impression on his heart, and he felt sure that her gentleness, and the good sense and piety of her parents, would prevent their feeling annoyance; he was too proud perhaps to venture; and the words which he often longed to say, were for ever unspoken.

HER END WAS PEACE

Years rolled on, and Pierre and Madeleine de l'Orme were gathered to their fathers. They had been fondly loved by their children, and their loss was deeply mourned; their life had been one of vicissitude, but they were spared to see their children settled and prospering in the world. Gaston had been apprenticed to a merchant in the city; and being a steady lad, he became a favourite with his master, who some years afterwards took him into partnership, and finally gave him his only daughter in marriage. They had a numerous family, but all their children died young, with the exception of one daughter, who married, and dying childless, that branch of the de l'Orme family became extinct. Marie and Madeleine both married pastors of the Reformed Church, countrymen of their own; and after a time, they both followed their husbands to Switzerland, where their descendants probably live at this day. Old Marthe died many years before her beloved master and mistress; she had been a good and faithful servant, and she was regretted as if she had been one of the family.

Little now remains to be told. Suzanne de l'Orme and her brother Jean survived their relatives a long time, the latter living considerably beyond the 'three score years and ten' usually allotted to man. As to Suzanne – the little Suzanne of our tale, it pleased God to prolong her existence to extreme old age. Had she lived a few weeks longer she would have completed her one hundredth year. She was to the last moment in full possession of her faculties, with the exception of her hearing, which became a little dulled, but not sufficiently so to be a source of discomfort. She retained her gentleness and sweetness of disposition to the end, and was an object of veneration and love to all who had the privilege of knowing her; and although she outlived all the members of her family, she never felt the want of friends.

Truly she enjoyed God's special protection and favour. He had seen fit in His wisdom to try her faith and obedience but with His help she had withstood every temptation, and remained firm and unshaken under trials which would have overcome many of maturer years. He had afflicted her with personal deformity, and she had borne this meekly and without complaint; she knew that 'God orders all things well,' and although there were moments when the sight of the happiness of others brought a pang to her affectionate and loving heart, since her affliction debarred her from enjoying such happiness; yet her good sense, and reliance on her Almighty Father, soon brought back rest and submission to her well-balanced mind.

She bowed to a long and solitary life. Her days were spent in works of usefulness and charity, and she never murmured at what God had ordered for her. Those scenes through which she had passed during her childhood were never removed from her mind. She loved to recall the mercies which had been showered on her during that period.

Her conversation had an especial charm to young people;

they delighted to hear her talk of the old days, during which she had experienced such extraordinary adventures, and as she never boasted of her steadfastness and courage, or uncharitably of her persecutors, her youthful listeners gained many a lesson of faith and humility which were never forgotten.

Hers was a character of intrinsic worth, but she had not attained to those virtues and qualities without much prayer and watchfulness. None but God knew of the struggles she had with herself to combat the weaknesses to which she was subject. Little by little she attained that peace of mind which was her comfort during the course of her long life.

At length the end came. For some days before her death, Mademoiselle de l'Orme felt a sensation of weakness stealing over her, and she instinctively knew that the Great Reaper was at hand. Joyfully, but patiently, she awaited His coming; when the summons came she was ready – and so she passed away! So gently, that the loving friends who watched beside her couch, scarcely could tell when she drew her last breath. Her long life had come to a close – her warfare was ended – she had fought the good fight – and she had entered into the joy of her Lord! Her end was peace!

THE END.

Classic Fiction Titles

Little Faith
A little girl learns to trust
O. F. Walton

Faith, persecuted by her
grandmother when her
mother dies,
finds faith and justice.

ISBN: 1 85792 567X

Christie's Old Organ
A little boy's journey to find a home of his own
O. F. Walton

Christie is a street child. He
sets out with Treffy,
the organ grinder,
to find a place of peace.

ISBN: 1 85792 5238

Classic Fiction Titles

A Peep Behind the Scenes
A little girl's journey of discovery
O. F. Walton

Rosalie is forced from place to place with her brutal father's travelling theatre - if only she could find a real loving relationship?
ISBN: 1 85792 5246

Pilgrim's Progress
John Bunyan

Christian leaves the doomed City of Destruction and under the orders of Evangelist travels towards the Heavenly City.
ISBN: 1 845501020

CHRISTIAN FOCUS PUBLICATIONS

Christian Focus | Christian Heritage | CF4K | Mentor

Christian Focus Publications publishes books for adults and children under its three main imprints: Christian Focus, Mentor and Christian Heritage. Our books reflect that God's word is reliable and Jesus is the way to know him, and live for ever with him.

Our children's publication list includes a Sunday school curriculum that covers pre-school to early teens; puzzle and activity books. We also publish personal and family devotional titles, biographies and inspirational stories that children will love.

If you are looking for quality Bible teaching for children then we have an excellent range of Bible story and age specific theological books.

From pre-school to teenage fiction, we have it covered!

**Find us at our web page:
www. christianfocus. com**

CF4•K
*Because you're never
to young to know Jesus*